**The Witch of Goingsnake
and Other Stories**

The Witch of Goingsnake and Other Stories

By Robert J. Conley

Foreword by Wilma P. Mankiller
Principal Chief of the Cherokee Nation

University of Oklahoma Press
Norman and London

By Robert J. Conley

(Editor) *A Return to Vision*, with Richard Cherry and Bernard Hirsch (Boston, 1971)
(Editor) *Poems for Comparison and Contrast*, with Richard Cherry (New York, 1972)
(Editor) *The Shadow Within*, with Richard Cherry and Bernard Hirsch (Boston, 1973)
(Editor) *A Return to Vision* (2d ed.), with Richard Cherry and Bernard Hirsch (Boston, 1974) (Boston, 1975)
(Editor) *Echoes of Our Being* (Muskogee, Okla., 1982)
The Rattlesnake Band and Other Poems (Muskogee, Okla., 1984)
Back to Malachi (New York, 1986)
The Actor (New York, 1987)

Library of Congress Cataloging-in-Publication Data
Conley, Robert J.
  The witch of Goingsnake and other stories.
  1. Cherokee Indians—Fiction. I. Title.
PS3553.0494W5 1988   813'.54   88–4762
ISBN 0–8061–2148–3 (cloth)
ISBN 0–8061–2353–2 (pbk.)

The paper in this book meets the guidelines for permanence and durability of the Committee on Production Guidelines for Book Longevity of the Council on Library Resources, Inc. ⊚

for Wesley Proctor
and for all who knew and loved him

Contents

	Page
Foreword, by Wilma P. Mankiller, Principal Chief of the Cherokee Nation	ix
A Note to the Reader	xi
Acknowledgments	xv
Yellow Bird: An Imaginary Autobiography	3
The Immortals	38
Wili Woyi	43
The Night George Wolfe Died	68
Wickliffe	71
The Hanging of Mose Miller	80
The Witch of Goingsnake	86
Moon Face	101
The Name	105
The Mexican Tattoo	114
Badger	124
Calf Roper's House Guest	131
Calf Roper's Bandit Car	139
Bob Parris's Temper	143
His Grandma's Wedding	146
Old Joe	148
Wesley's Story	152
The Endless Dark of the Night	159

Foreword

By Wilma P. Mankiller

Several significant works have been published about the political history of the Cherokee people, the hostilities of the eighteenth century, the tragic forced removal in the early and middle nineteenth century, the rapid advances in the late nineteenth century, and the rebirth of the Cherokee Nation in present times.

We Cherokee have sustained many losses in the last three hundred years of contact with non-Indians. Despite these losses we have retained a strong cultural heritage, the language given to us by the Creator, and many of our ancient traditions. One of those ancient traditions, preserved so well by Robert Conley, is the art of storytelling.

There are few contemporary Cherokee writers who can communicate the stories and values of Cherokee society. There are even fewer who can equal Robert Conley in translating the stories passed down from generation to generation since the beginning of time.

While reading this collection of stories, I was reminded again and again of the words Cherokee author/composer Jack Kilpatrick used in describing Cherokee life. "Balance and synthesis, and the acceptance of the nonmaterial nature of Cherokee existence lie at the foundation of the Cherokee thought world."

The Witch of Goingsnake and Other Stories gives the reader a rare glimpse into the culture of the Cherokee people. All of the stories in this collection have an important value lesson. The story of the origin of Thunder provided my family with an evening's discussion of the natural world. *The Night George Wolfe Died* depicts the continual struggle of the Cherokee to succeed in the "white man's world" while maintaining a Cherokee belief system and way of life. In the early nineteenth century, the Cherokee made a tremendous effort to adapt to the white man's world. Many believed that those efforts would protect the Cherokee from adverse action by the U.S. government. Indeed, it had no effect at all. As in George Wolfe's case, the business suits, education, and advancement did not matter. It mattered only that we were Cherokee. The forced removal of our people, who stood in the way of gold-hungry settlers, from their home in the Southeast to Indian Territory, now Oklahoma, is a dark testament to that fact.

Much has been written about the Cherokee people. Not enough has been written by the Cherokee people. The subtle nuances of language, the memories of tribal life, and the strong sense of the past and its integration with the present are lost even to the most gifted non-Cherokee writer. There is a movement among contemporary Cherokee writers to produce more indigenous literature. Robert Conley is a leader of that movement.

Finally, I must convey a story of my own regarding Robert Conley and this collection of stories. Recently I sat beneath a brush arbor at a Cherokee stomp grounds talking with Julie Moss, a Cherokee poet. I conveyed to her my great pleasure in reading this collection of Conley's stories. I concluded that Robert Conley is a writer with such perception that he could make drinking a cup of coffee seem . . . (I grasped for words). Julie finished by saying, " . . . spiritual." That, I believe, is the essence of Robert Conley's gift.

A Note to the Reader

When the editors at the University of Oklahoma Press first asked me whether I would like to write an introduction to this collection of stories, I declined, probably out of a sense that the stories should stand by and for themselves, and partly from a false sense of modesty. I did not want to seem to be praising my own stories. On reflection I decided that perhaps I should offer up some comments about the stories, my purposes in writing them, and my sense of their place in a larger context than that of this volume.

I believe that many of our Native American tribal traditions are vital. That is to say, they are alive in all the manifestations of culture. More specifically, our tribal literary traditions are alive and continuing. The tribal literary tradition with which I am particularly concerned is that of the Cherokee people, and I am conscious that the stories included in this collection grow out of and are a part of that tribal tradition. In her foreword to this book, Principal Chief Wilma Mankiller insists that we Cherokees "have retained a strong cultural heritage" and that one of the well-preserved traditions of that heritage "is the art of storytelling." She makes further reference to "a movement among contemporary Cherokee writers to produce more indigenous literature" and assigns to me a prominent and flattering position in that movement.

All of this carries with it a major implication for readers of this collection, particularly, I expect, for non-Cherokee readers. These stories do not grow out of European literary traditions so much as they do out of those of the Cherokee. Behind these stories are gathered a whole set of cultural referents, a different way of interpreting events, a different notion of time, a different concept of language, and, of course, a different view of the purpose and art of storytelling. In short, a non-Cherokee, especially a non-Indian, reader of this collection should be prepared to deal with an unfamiliar world view.

I do not want to fall into the trap of offering up analyses of my own fiction. I think that, if that sort of thing should be done at all, it is best left to others. I would, however, like to offer a few specific examples from my stories of the generalities I mentioned above.

The American Indian concept of time is cyclical as opposed to the European/white American concept of linear time. In a sense there is no past, no future. All things are present. Thus when my fictionalized Ridge, or Yellow Bird, tells his story, even though he moves structurally from the ancient tales to a brief outline of history to a poetic interpretation of history to a family history and finally to his own personal history, there is still a sense of confused chronology. There are repeated events. There is no clear distinction between past and present.

In American Indian societies, Cherokee included, the sense of community is much stronger than the sense of the worth of the individual. Individual worth is defined in a community context. Simon Ortiz, asked in 1972 to submit a brief biographical statement to *Pembroke Magazine* for an issue that would include some of his poetry, wrote, "First of all, I'm Acoma, only then am I anything else." And when Geronimo, while held prisoner at Fort Sill, was approached by Lawton, Oklahoma, school teacher S. N. Barret for his life story, the old warrior began by relating the Apache tribal creation story. Thus, Ridge's "imaginary autobiography" combines his own life story with Cherokee history and oral tradition. His claim that his "life in itself is of little moment" is more than simple modesty. It is a basic part of the Cherokee view of what is important—community rather than individuality.

The American Indian spirit world does not exist as a world apart from the real world. The world we inhabit in this life is both physical and spiritual. To Cherokees, as to other American Indians, spirit life is an everyday reality. Though Wili Woyi's story never actually says that Wili Woyi became invisible, it clearly gives the impression that he did exactly that. Other stories contain examples of what might be called "Indian medicine," or even "magic." In the context of Cherokee culture these stories are not fantasies; they are stories about reality—the reality known to Cherokees.

Storytelling to American Indians traditionally is more than entertainment and more than education. It is vital and necessary to continued life—the life of the tribe and the life of the world itself. Creation stories are told ritually to ensure the continued existence of the world. And, as is beautifully expressed by Dr. N. Scott Momaday (Kiowa) in his widely published speech, "The Man Made of Words," a people is without identity until it has imagined itself one and has given that imagined identity form through the art of storytelling. Ridge's story, his life, and his identity (that is, his character) are all one. Cherokee Bill, the young man who grew up outside of the culture, only nominally Cherokee, has no real sense of identity until he imagines himself a Cherokee, an act that is not complete until he has an appropriate name—Cherokee Bill. And though Bennie is still wondering about his place in the world at the end of the story "Wickliffe," it is the newspaper account's completion of the story of Charlie Wickliffe and Deputy Marshal Gilstrap that sets him to wondering.

I will admit to being a writer who is not always conscious of a purpose in writing a given story beyond that of telling a good story. I will, however, confess here to a purpose in putting together this particular selection of stories into a collection. I wanted to show not only something of the range of Cherokee history but also something of the variety within contemporary Cherokee culture. When we speak of the Cherokee people today, we are speaking of a people whose ranks include both full-blood and mixed-blood people, both traditional and assimilated people, and a tremendous range of variations between those extremes. There is a vast cultural difference between Wili Woyi and Cherokee Bill, or even between Badger and Calf Roper. Yet these characters all have one thing in common. They are Cherokee. Someone once said of the Cherokee people that you can find Cherokees who will say that they don't use Cherokee medicine, but you can't find a Cherokee who will say, "I don't believe in it." This, I think, is aptly illustrated by the final story in this collection, "The Endless Dark of the Night."

ROBERT J. CONLEY

Sioux City, Iowa

Acknowledgments

"The Night George Wolfe Died" first appeared in *Indian Voice Magazine* 2, no. 3 (May/June 1972).

"The Witch of Goingsnake" first appeared in *Sun Tracks: An American Indian Literary Magazine* 3, no. 1 (Fall 1976).

"Wili Woyi" first appeared in *The Remembered Earth: An Anthology of Contemporary Native American Literature.* Edited by Geary Hobson. Albuquerque: Red Earth Press, 1979. (Reissued by the University of New Mexico Press, 1981.)

"The Immortals" first appeared in the *Iowa Archeological Society Newsletter,* no. 111 (Summer 1984).

"Wesley's Story" first appeared in *The Greenfield Review* 12, nos. 1, 2 (Summer/Fall 1984).

"The Endless Dark of the Night," reprinted with permission from *Earth Power Coming: Short Fiction in Native American Literature,* Navajo Community College Press, 1983.

R. J. C.

The Witch of Goingsnake
and Other Stories

Yellow Bird:
An Imaginary Autobiography

The year is 1867. I am forty years old, and I am writing from Grass Valley, in the state of California—the state called by my people Adel' juhdluh, "They get money from out of there." I am lying in what I know will soon be my death bed. The physicians have diagnosed my illness as "a softening of the brain," but I alone know its source. I am in no pain, although I have gone through much intense suffering. It has passed, however, and now I am calm and reasonably comfortable. I am weak and I know that I am dying, but my mind and body alike are reconciled to the inevitable. My only regret is for my poor wife, Elizabeth. She will suffer greatly, for I know that she loves me, and I know that she will never understand what has happened to me, much less the reasons underlying my— and her—present circumstances. I am much to blame, for I should never have convinced the poor woman to share a miserable life with me. But soon she will be set free, and I pray that she will in time overcome her grief and begin her life anew. My only hope for myself is for time and strength to finish this sorry tale before I am taken away to the Darkening Land.

The blood of two races flows in my veins. My mother, Sarah Bird Northrup, was of a good, old Connecticut family, a white woman whose parents strenuously objected to her marriage to my father. My father, known to the world as John Ridge, was named *Skah-tle-loh-skee* in the Cherokee language. When I was born, I was given two names—John Rollin Ridge and Tsisqua Dahlonageh—according to current Cherokee practice. The latter name means "Yellow Bird," or, because English is backward to Cherokee, "Bird Yellow."

To be totally honest and forthright, I should mention that had I been born at an earlier time in history I could not justifiably claim my father's heritage as my own. I could not, that is, claim my own Cherokee blood, because under our ancient traditions a child belongs to its mother and, by extension, to her clan. Since my mother was a white woman, I have no clan. Some years ago a man without a clan could not be a Cherokee except by adoption into a clan. However, at about the time of my birth our Nation adopted the manner, customs, and style of European nations. I was born a Cherokee citizen under the Cherokee Constitution and laws, and I was brought up among my people—the Cherokee people. I have ever been Cherokee, and whatever befalls me in the future, I shall ever remain Cherokee.

But perhaps I have started ahead of my story. My life in itself is of little moment, and it would be a monstrous presumption on my part to present the world with the story of my life as something to take note of were it not for the fact that my story is a part of the story of my people. A man does not exist alone and apart, though in times of trial it may seem so. I am a Cherokee, and my story is of the Cherokees.

At the time of my birth, in 1827, in what is now called the state of Georgia, the Cherokees were living in our ancient homelands. The land has now been taken from us and carved up into the states of Georgia, North and South Carolina, Tennessee, Kentucky, Alabama, and West Virginia. It is a mountainous country and heavily wooded. It is a beautiful land, and though it was stolen from us, it is Cherokee land, for it has been nourished for hundreds, perhaps thousands, of years by the flesh and blood of Cherokee people, and Cherokee spirits will forever inhabit its hills and valleys.

This is how the old ones tell us that the world is made: Everything that we know, the world in which we exist, was originally covered by water. But there are two other worlds, and they have always existed. They are spiritual worlds inhabited by spiritual beings. One is beneath us, and its seasons are exactly opposite ours. It is chaotic and unpredictable—a world in which anything can happen— a world in which the unexpected is commonplace. The other world is above us, atop a great Sky-Vault made of rock. It is calm, orderly, and predictable. Neither of these worlds is either good or bad, but because their powerful spiritual forces are exactly opposite one another, there exists a constant and tremendous spiritual conflict between them, and this world on which we live and breathe and go about our daily chores is set directly in the center of that turmoil. Our task, we are told, is to live our lives in such a way as to maintain a constant and precarious balance between these powerful opposing forces.

The stories that are told, a few of which I shall here relate, lay down the rules of life. They tell us where we came from, how to live, and why. They constitute our Bible, if you will, and lately I have given them much thought. For years they had not been much with me, having been replaced by the dogma of the missionaries. Perhaps that is the whole source of the troubles, and perhaps, if you read my story through, you will begin to understand.

Once, they say, there was no middle world, but only water. All forms of life we know on earth today, and even some we know no longer, existed in their primal forms on high. They lived atop the Sky-Vault. The life forms on the Sky-Vault became too populous, so they looked around for someplace else to go. They came to the water of the middle world, where, of course, they could not stand. They wondered if perhaps there might be something down beneath the water. Dayunisi (Beaver's Grandchild), the water beetle, volunteered to go down and see. He dived headlong into the waters, and he was gone so long that the others thought him lost. They had given up hope for his return and were about to leave when he emerged and brought forth from the depths some mud. They spread the mud on the surface of the water; then, to dry it so they could stand on it, the Great Buzzard flew back and forth, flapping his wings. The motion of his wings as he flew close to the mud created the mountains and the valleys of the land the Cherokees would learn to love.

The time or space that followed was what we know in Cherokee as the Ancient Time, the time in which the universal rules were made. The first man and woman, for instance, had plenty to eat, and they had perfect health, but then, they say, some things took place that changed all that, and the universal laws were made that apply to all of us for all time to come.

The first man was called Kanati, the Perfect Hunter, and his wife was Selu, Corn. They had one son. Everyday Kanati brought home fresh game, and everyday Selu had fresh corn and beans. One day Selu washed off some meat in the river that ran near their house. A few days later their son went out to play, and he went to the river. After a while Kanati and Selu heard the voices of two boys at play. When their son came home, they asked him about the other voice.

"A boy came out to play with me," he said, "and he said that he's my brother."

"Then bring him home with you tomorrow," the mother said.

Next day after play the boy came home alone.

"He wouldn't come," he said. "He said that you threw him away."

Then Selu knew that he had grown from the blood of the meat she had washed in the river.

"Tomorrow when you go to play," Kanati said, "your mother and I will follow and hide. Wrestle with him and hold him down and then call out to us."

The next day the boy did as he was told, and when he got the other boy down, he called his parents out.

"We don't want to hurt you," said Kanati.

"Come home with us. We'll care for you," said Selu.

But the strange boy struggled to get free.

"Let me go," he cried. "You threw me away."

At last, however, they prevailed upon him and took him home. They found him to be so mischievous that they called him the Wild Boy. And the Wild Boy constantly led his brother into mischief and trouble.

The two boys followed their father to hunt one day, though he had strictly forbidden them to do so. They hid and watched as he moved a large rock from in front of a cave. Out ran a deer. Kanati quickly shot the deer and put the rock back in place. He shouldered the deer and headed for home. The boys ran fast to move the rock, and when they did the deer came running out. The boys were nearly trampled by the stampede of the deer. And the deer were followed by other animals: raccoons, foxes, wolves, and 'possums, even buffalo (a few), and, finally, the birds. So many birds came out that the sky was black, and the noise of their wings was tremendous.

Kanati heard the commotion, and he rushed back to the cave. He saw what his boys had done and in a rage went into the cave and kicked over some jars. Bees, mosquitoes, wasps, gnats, and all kinds of flying, buzzing insects swarmed from the jars and out of the cave and began stinging and biting the two bad boys. They ran. They swatted. They screamed. They fell to the ground rolling over and over. At last Kanati drove the swarms away.

Because of what the boys did, the game was all let loose, and hunters now must work much harder on the hunt to bring home game.

One day not too long after that, Kanati brought home no meat. Selu was not upset. She went outside behind the house to a shed, and she returned again with a large basket filled with corn and beans. The Wild Boy watched her intently, and then he pulled aside his brother.

"Where does our mother get all that food?" he asked.

The next time they needed corn and beans, the boys ran and hid behind the shed and found a crack in the wall and peeked through. As they watched, Selu got down on her knees in the center of the floor. She placed the large basket in front of her knees. She rubbed her stomach with her hands, and the basket was filled with corn. She rubbed her sides below her arms, and beans filled the basket to overflowing. Wild Boy whispered to his brother.

"Our mother is a witch, and we must kill her."

They ran and got an axe and waited for her just inside the house. When Selu stepped inside the doorway and saw the boys, she knew just what they had in mind.

"I see that you bad boys intend to kill your mother," she said.

"We watched you," said the Wild Boy, "and we know that you're a witch."

"First listen to what I have to say so that when I am gone you will still have food to eat."

She told the boys that after they had done their deed, they should clear a space in the shape of a circle in front of the house. Then they should drag her body seven times across it. In the morning they would have ripe corn to eat. The boys killed her, and they cleared the space, but, tired of the dragging, they failed to do it seven times. Because of that the corn takes longer to mature and must be tended carefully. Just like the hunters, farmers today have a harder life because of those two boys.

When Kanati returned and saw what the boys had done, he left them and went back to his original home on the Sky-Vault in the West in a place called the Darkening Land. There he found Selu, his wife, awaiting him. But the two bad boys even followed him there. And today Kanati is Thunder, whom we also call Gigage Asgaya, or

Red Man, and the boys are the Little Thunders or the Thunder Boys.

From time to time, Thunder returned to this world for visits, and often when he did, he left behind a woman pregnant with his child. One such woman never married. She raised her child, a son, alone, and as the boy grew he developed ugly sores over all his body. He was ashamed and stayed in the house all the time.

One day his mother took pity on his condition, and she called him to her.

"I never told you this before," she said, "but your father is Thunder. He is a great doctor, and I know he can cure you."

She made her son some new clothes, made him some parched corn, and sent him on his way.

"Thunder lives to the west," she said.

The boy traveled for many days and nights. Everywhere he found anyone, he asked the way to Thunder's house.

"To the west," they always said.

At last he came to a house owned by a man called Untsaiyi. This name means "Brass," and the man was made of brass, but he was also called the Gambler. Brass had invented a gambling game, which we call Gatayusti. It is played on a large, round field, and Brass's playing field was there in front of his house. As the boy approached the house, he found Brass in his playing field with his stone wheel and his throwing stick.

"Hello there, boy," said Brass. "Come on and play a game with me."

"Hello. I haven't time," replied the boy. "I'm looking for the house of Thunder. Can you tell me how far it is?"

"Why, your journey is almost over," said Brass. "He lives just over that hill. I hear him every now and then rumbling away. Play me a game before you go."

"No. I really have to hurry on. Besides, I have nothing to bet."

"I'll play for your pretty spots," said Brass.

The boy's cheeks grew hot and flushed, for he knew that Brass was making fun of his sores.

"I have to go," he said, "but I'll stop and play you on my way back."

Now, word had come to Thunder that the boy was coming. Thunder knew he had left some sons behind in the middle world, but he had a suspicious mind. Any boy would like to say he was Thunder's son.

"I'll have to test this boy," he thought.

So when the boy arrived, Thunder told him to sit down and showed him a chair. The chair was made of long, sharp thorns, but Thunder had it covered with a blanket so the boy wouldn't know. The boy sat on the chair and was comfortable. Thunder stroked his chin and watched.

"Perhaps this is my boy," he thought.

"What is it that you want of me?" he said out loud.

"My mother told me that you are my father," the boy said. "She also told me that you are a great doctor. I came to ask you to cure me of these sores."

"I can do that," Thunder said.

He called his wife and had her build a fire and set a pot of water on to boil. Then Thunder got some herbs and threw them in the water and let them boil awhile. Then he picked up the boy. The boy showed no fear, and when Thunder dropped him into the pot of boiling water, he showed no pain.

"Carry this pot down to the stream," Thunder told his wife, "and throw it in."

She did. She threw the heavy pot, with boiling water, herbs, boy and all into the stream, and when it hit, a giant cloud of steam went up. The stream began to boil. And when the stream cleared, the boy was in the water, clinging to the roots of a tree growing on the bank. His spots were gone. Then Thunder's wife gave him a hand and helped him out of the water. With his sores gone, the boy was handsome.

"Listen to me," said Thunder's wife. "Your father is suspicious. He has more tests for you, but while we walk back to the house, I will tell you what to expect and what to do."

When they arrived back at the house, the boy was prepared.

"Well," said Thunder, "you look new. You need some new clothes."

He gave the boy a new deerskin dress and had him put it on. Then he placed a large box in the center of the room and told the boy to pick his ornaments from there. The boy looked into the box and saw that it was filled with writhing snakes. He shoved his arm into the box all the way to the botton (as he had been told to do) and pulled out what he found there. It was a rattlesnake. He wrapped it around his neck for a necklace. He reached in again and brought out a copperhead, which he put on his right arm for a bracelet. A third time he plunged his arm into the box, and he brought out another copperhead. This one he put on his left arm.

"Now," said Thunder, "I want you to play ball with your brothers."

He handed the boy two ballsticks and sent him to the field. There the Thunder Boys showed up. And as the game progressed, the Thunder cracked and rolled, and then, as the new boy ran back and forth across the field, the lightning began to flash, for the boy was Thunder's son, and he was Lightning.

When Lightning tired of the game, he struck a tree beside the field (Thunder's wife had told him of this tree— Thunder's favorite), and Thunder stopped the game for fear the Lightning would kill his favorite tree.

Then Lightning told his father of the promise he had made to stop and play a game with Brass, the Gambler. But Thunder was acquainted with the Gambler.

"He cheats," he said. "He can't bear to lose. But he won't be able to beat you, and you'll have an endless string of beads to bet."

He gave Lightning a gourd with a hole in its end and a string of beads dangling out through the hole.

"He will bet more and more each time he loses until he will bet his own life. Still you will win. Then call your brothers to help you kill him."

Lightning went to the home of Brass and found him waiting there ready to play. Lightning began walking around the field, pulling the string of beads from the gourd. At last the beads encircled the playing field and still there was no end to the string. Brass wanted that gourd. But every time he rolled his stone and Lightning threw his stick, when the stone stopped rolling and the point of the stick sank into the ground, the stone and the stick were touching. Finally Brass had nothing left to bet.

"We'll play for my wife against your beads," he said.

He lost again.

"Another game," he said. "If I lose this time you can kill me."

And Lightning won the game.

"Just let me go inside my house and tell my wife what's happened here," said Brass.

Brass went inside, but he didn't come back. Lightning went inside the house and found a back door opened. He called his brothers, who came with their dog, but the dog was a beetle. They all got on the trail of Brass. When they had gone a ways, they came across an old man sitting beside the road carving a pipe from stone. They told him they were following the trail of Brass.

"He hasn't been by here," the old man said. "I've been here all day at my work."

Just then the beetle flew high into the air and made a fast dive straight for the old man's head. It struck him hard in the center of the forehead and bounced off with a ping. The beetle's head was green where it had struck the old man's head, and a spot of brass showed through the brown of the old man's skin. Then, there before their eyes, the old man became Brass, and he ran. The boys and the dog ran after him, but Brass ran fast and soon was out of sight.

12

The boys slowed down, and as they walked along the road, they saw an old woman standing there.

"Have you seen Brass go by this way?" they asked.

"No," she said, "and if he had come by this way, I would have surely seen him. I've been here all day long."

The beetle made his dive again and hit again with a ping. The old woman changed into Brass and ran, but this time the boys stayed close behind. Soon they came to the edge of the world. There was nothing beyond but water. The boys drove a long, sharp stake through the Gambler's chest, ran with him into the water and pinned him there to the ocean floor. They say that Brass will be there until the end of the world, because he cannot die.

Now here's what happened on another trip that Thunder made to the middle world. One time, still in those Ancient Times, a Cherokee boy went out to hunt. He was deep in the woods far from his home when he heard a tremendous commotion like the sounds of giant trees cracking, breaking, and crashing to the ground. There were very loud growling and scuffling sounds. And there was popping and cracking of Thunder. The boy looked in the direction of the sounds and saw coming from the far side of a hill a great cloud of dust and debris. He hurried to that hill and climbed it, and when he reached the top, this is what he saw.

There was a powerful and handsome man locked in a death struggle with a creature known as Uk'ten. The Uk'ten came from the lower world, and he was like a giant snake, but he had wings, and on his head were antlers. Fire came out of the Uk'ten's mouth, and on his forehead was a great and shiny crystal. They say that he could kill a man with a look or with his breath. When the boy came over the hill, the Uk'ten saw him and saw that he carried a bow and some arrows.

"Boy," the Uk'ten cried, "shoot this man for me and I'll forever be your friend."

But the man shouted out to the boy, "Don't listen to this

13

Uk'ten. If you kill me for him, he'll just kill you. Shoot him instead, and you'll have me for a friend."

The boy shot an arrow, and it sank into the Uk'ten's flesh but did no harm.

"Shoot him in the seventh spot," the man said.

The boy looked, and sure enough, the Uk'ten had seven spots along his body. The boy took aim again and this time sent his arrow right into the seventh spot. The Uk'ten roared and writhed in pain, then went rolling down the hill, ripping up all the trees in his path until finally he came to rest at the bottom of the hill—still and dead.

The man whom the boy saved was Thunder, and because of what the boy did, Thunder has always been a friend of the Cherokees.

There are many other stories about the Ancient Time that tell us how things came to be the way they are, how we should conduct our lives, and how to maintain the balance in this world. I heard these stories many times as a child, and they have helped to shape my character, even though I pushed them to the back of my mind for a number of years. As I have said, I heard the ancient stories, told by the old ones, many times as a child, but the world of the Cherokees was changing rapidly at the time of my birth. I was taught by the missionaries, as was my father. My Grandfather Ridge had grown to manhood under the ancient ways, but he had consciously rejected them and eagerly embraced what he called the civilizing influence of the white man. I was told the story of Adam and Eve and taught that all men came from their union. I was taught to believe that our ancient tales were nothing but childish fancy. I was taught, in short, that our entire ancient civilization was childlike. And Grandfather Ridge was determined that his offspring would be "Christian" and "civilized." It was during this time that he took the English translation of his Cherokee name, "I Came Walking Along the Ridge" and changed it into an English surname, Ridge. For a Christian name he later took the rank he had earned fighting in the white man's army, and he became Major Ridge. He gave his children Christian names (my father was John), after the style of the white man, and, usurping the power of the clan matron, he made himself the head of his family.

So the ancient tales, though known to me, were known as fairy tales, while the white man's Bible was known as the Word of God. And the old men who told the tales in earnest, who continued to dance and sing the old songs, were spoken of in our home as ignorant and superstitious. And the conjurers, whose power was still feared by my venerable grandfather, so far as any belief in their power was retained, were believed to be in league with the forces of Satan.

So the world of the Cherokees became two worlds, and the delicate balance, which had been maintained for so long, was lost. There were some who fought bravely and desperately to regain the balance and even forfeited their lives for the effort, and yet they lost. Those on the opposite side were convinced that salvation for the Cherokees lay at the end of the white man's road. They too fought and died—and they, too, lost. And here is the way it came about.

Neither my strength nor my knowledge will allow me to chronicle the entire history of the Cherokee people, but I cannot tell my own story without at least a summary of the major events that led up to it. Do not lose patience with me or think that I am delirious. My mind is clear, more so, perhaps, than ever before in my life, and everything that I am writing is related to my present condition —is a part of my impending death. The chronicle that follows is a tale of the loss of balance and the chaos that resulted from that loss, and though white man's blood, too, flows in my veins, I believe that the loss was caused by the entry of the white man into our precarious world. The major events in this story are chronicled below.

The Cherokee people lived in about fifty towns throughout the land that now makes up parts of North Carolina,

South Carolina, Georgia, Alabama, Kentucky, West Virginia, and Tennessee. They walked in balance.

1540: Europeans visited our land. They were Spaniards, led by De Soto. We welcomed them and gave them dogs to eat. We called them *ayonega*, or *yonegs*, "white people."

1673: The English came. They came from a colony they had established, called Virginia.

1693: The English sold some Cherokees, just as they did blacks and cattle, as slaves.

1711: We fought the Tuscaroras. Then we discovered, along with the Tuscaroras, that the *yonegs* had tricked us both into the war. We fought the *yonegs*.

1715: Again we had a war with them—the whites.

1721: The *yonegs* took some land from us.

1736: A little man from England, whose name was Coming, talked our leaders into designating one man "Emperor" of all the Cherokees. This was agreed upon because the English liked to have only one man with whom to deal on matters of trade and treaties. We agreed for those purposes, but the English never understood that he was not an emperor in the sense that they understood the word. The man so designated was named Amaedohi, meaning "the Water Walker." The English wrote his name down in their books as "Moytoy."

1738: The *yonegs* gave us smallpox. One-half our people died.

1761: We had another war with them.

1771: My grandfather was born. He was called, for a time, Nung-noh-hut-tah-hee, or "He Who Slays the Enemy in the Path." In English this name is usually called "Pathkiller." Later his name became Kah-nung-dah-clah-geh, because of my grandfather's frequent statement, "I Came Along the Top of the Mountain." It was this latter name that he eventually modified to "Ridge."

1773: The *yoneg* missionaries came and told us we were praying to the devil. We did not even know the devil.

1775: Some of our chiefs gave in to pressures from the whites and sold some of our land. One of the whites involved was Daniel Boone, and he made money speculating on that land. One of our greatest patriots, Dragging Canoe, and his followers, known as the Chickamaugans, believing that land to still be ours, fought with the *yonegs* from that day until he died.

1783: They sent us smallpox yet again and wiped out many more of our people.

1785: The Treaty of Hopewell established peace between the Cherokees and the newly formed United States. It was the first of many treaties that nation would demand of us. They took more land, and they promised to remove the whites who had squatted on our land. They never kept that promise.

1791: The Treaty of Holston was signed. Three thousand whites were living on our land, and since the United States had failed to keep its promise, Dragging Canoe fought to drive them out. The new treaty established peace again, took more of our land, provided some payment for it, repeated the same promise regarding whites on Indian land, and made provisions to lead the Cherokees "to a greater degree of civilization."

1792: Dragging Canoe died that year.

1794: Chief Bowl and others who were dissatisfied with the encroachment of the whites onto our lands went to Arkansas. Then they went to Texas, where many of them, including Bowl, were later killed.

1801: The Moravians established a mission school amongst us.

1802: President Jefferson signed an agreement with the state of Georgia promising to take from us all the lands which Georgia claimed. The Cherokees did not know about this agreement, but looking on it today, we can see that the U.S. Government deliberately deceived us with every treaty we signed after that date, for they agreed with us in treaties to leave us in peace forever on our remaining lands.

1807: Grandfather Ridge was selected by the Cherokee National Council as one of the men to execute Doublehead, one of our town chiefs, for having betrayed our people and sold our land.

1808: Tahlonteskee and other Cherokees moved west to Arkansas. We call them the Old Settlers.

1813: Grandfather Ridge became Major Ridge while fighting in the army of Andrew Jackson against the Creek Red Sticks. Other Cherokees fought with Jackson in that war.

1821: Sequoyah gave our people the syllabary with which to write in Cherokee.

1822: Our Nation established a Supreme Court.

1827: I was born. In this same year the Cherokee Nation adopted its first written constitution and elected John Ross as its principal chief.

That completes my outline of the history of the Cherokee people up until the date of my birth. Here I will insert some verse on the same subject, which I have on hand but have never published.

The Migrations of the Cherokees

1.

The Migration of Legend

Once, in times to history lost, they say,
a large group of Cherokees found their way
across the Mississippi, there—somewhere—
to make new homes, but legend says that there,
in the west, in the place of darkness, they
can but wander. Forever lost their way.
For in the west dwells death, and even the Sun
dies there, but the first migration was done.

2.

Chief Bowl

For twenty years in seventeen-ninety-four
the Cherokees and whites had been at war—
had fought with one another, when Chief Bowl,
with a small band, captured at Muscle Shoals
the boat of William Scott and killed that day
six men and took for captives for his pay
three women, four children, twenty-one slaves.
Bowl knew his success would be met with waves
of indignation from the other chiefs,
for they were engaged at the time in peace
talks with the whites. He led his men not home
but down the Tennessee, and then they roamed
west to the Saint Francis River, then more west
to Arkansas, before coming to rest
in Texas.   And these were not lost to those
back home in the east, as the others who chose,
according to legend, to go west had been.
They made their homes on the River Red, then
protected the Texans from Indians

who'd attack from the north, while Mexicans
came from the south. In trade for this aid
Sam Houston, acting for Texas, made
a treaty with Bowl, which took the stand
of the Cherokees' right to live on the land.
Well, it wasn't the first time, nor was it
the last, that white men's words proved worth not a whit.
Texans elected Lamar in eighteen-
thirty-eight, and Mirabeau didn't mean
for Indians, not Cherokee nor any kind,
to live within the new republic's lines.
He sent an army to drive them across
the Red. The Cherokees suffered a loss,
and they moved again, but without their Chief:
Bowl lay dead in Texas, clutching the sheaf
of paper Houston'd signed.

3.

Tahlonteskee

                Meanwhile back east
the United States, growing like bread with yeast,
put pressure on the Cherokees to move
the entire Nation, to drop into the groove
already cut out for them in the west.
Some brothers had gone before: now the rest
should join them there. And the government urged
them to go. The white population surged
'round the Cherokee Nation. Land and game
were getting scarce.
             Then from Arkansas came
word from Bowl and his band: hunting was good:
the hilly land was covered with woods:
no white men were there. A leading chief,
Tahlonteskee, decided to seek the relief
of western wilderness.

                              (Besides, he had
with Chief Doublehead made a very bad
decision two years past by signing
his name to a treaty redefining
Cherokee boundaries in favor of whites.
Some had then killed Doublehead, and they might
do so to Tahlonteskee, too.)
                              He set out,
summer of eighteen-oh-nine, on a route,
with a few hundred folks, for Arkansas.

4.

John Jolly

In the east, the year eighteen-eighteen saw
around the Nation, which once covered vast
areas of Appalachia, a fast-
tightening band drawing close and closer 'til the guest had surrounded the host—
'til the once powerful Nation was confined
to a small area in North Carolina,
Tennessee, and Georgia.
                              On Hiwasee
Island, Houston's boyhood home, Oolooteskee,
foster father of the future father
of Texas, watched the growing fuss and bother
of white menace in his land. Oolooteskee,
he who was known to whites as John Jolly,
though loath to leave homeland, wanted more room.
He feared that already was sealed the doom
of the Nation.
                              Tahlonteskee, his brother,
had gone on before. Before he smother
under the rising white tide, perhaps he,
too, should move on. West, the traps would be
full once again.

Then came from Washington
an official visit from his foster son.
And even Houston thought it would be best
for John Jolly to lead his people west.
And so, persuaded by his son, Houston,
Chief Jolly took his people and moved them.

5.

The Treaty Party

And still continued the great debate
between the U.S. and the tiny state
of Cherokee. On one side the greedy
red-necks, wanting Indian land—seedy
people—have-nots who, since they had nothing,
wanted to steal from others to bring
themselves up out of the mire. And standing
firmly behind them also demanding
Cherokee dispossession were Lumpkin,
Georgia's governor, and another bumpkin
who'd made it big, Old Hickory himself,
Andrew Jackson.
     The Cherokees were elves
in the woods against the giant Jackson.
This man, once friend of the Raven, Houston,
rose to fame in war with Creeks, then turned
his back on those who'd helped him to the win—
 spurned
them for causes more politic. Judas
of the wilderness, or, at least, Brutus,
sat in the president's chair when Jackson
was loosed in the White House.
       But the Sun
had not yet set on the tiny Nation
of Cherokees, struggling to keep their station
in the east. There were voices strong raised in

their behalf—voices of men of reason,
compassion, and justice—voices which cried
that their country had lost its way—had lied
once again to steal land from the people
who lived on it first. There were Ralph Waldo
Emerson, David Crockett, Francis Scott
Key, three who tried hard to rub out the blot
that Jackson would smear on history's page.
The debate went to court, and there the sage
justice, Marshall, declared it illegal
for Lumpkin and Jackson to move the people
from their ancestral home.
                                        But Jackson's men
had persuaded certain Cherokees then
that removal west, though sad, would be
the wisest of moves for the Cherokee.
On the twenty-ninth day of December
(a day Cherokees all will remember),
in eighteen-and-thirty five, at a place
called New Echota, on treaty were traced
the following names: John Ridge and Major
Ridge, Elias Boudinot, James Starr, Sr.,
and Stand Watie. Though they had not the right
to speak for their Nation, there was the might
of Jackson which gave them authority.
So in spite of justice, morality,
and the highest court of the land, Jackson
ordered the army on down to pack them
out of the Nation.
                                And those who had signed
had agreed to go in very short time
to join the others out west. The trek
for the signers was not all that bleak;
they were helped on their way in exchange for
all the events their names had arranged for.
And when they left home, they took west with them
more of the people away from the din.

6.

The Trail of Tears

John Ross was Chief of the Cherokees, and
he and his followers stayed on the land.
They refused to allow that the treaty
signed at Echota had any validity.
In response, King Andy said that John Ross
was not the legal chief, and, as he was boss
of the U.S. Army, he sent it out
to corral all Cherokees, completely rout
them out of their homes and out of the hills.
In the meantime, Lumpkin loosed for the kill
red-necks from all over Georgia to take
what they wanted by force. Free to make
havoc, they did. Like a hungry wolf pack
with a peaceful fold of sheep to attack
and no watchful shepherd to interfere,
the red-necks descended. From front and rear
they raced in, and they lifted the cattle,
the sheep, and the pigs. It was no battle,
but ruffianism on a grand scale
sanctioned by Washington—a shameful tale—yet it is
    just begun.
                    The Cherokees
were hunted down and rounded up to be
placed in pens like wild animals until
the job was done. Who resisted was killed.
   There was one called Tsali, who told his sons
   to die on the land before being run
   west with the rest like cattle. A soldier,
   come to round them up, acted bolder
   than he ought—rudely pushed at Tsali's wife,
   pushed at her with bayonet, threat'ning life.
   In righteous indignation, Tsali struck
   down the wretch who dared so far push his luck
   as poke at Tsali's wife.

> Others found him,
> though, and took him in. They tried him, bound him,
> placed him before their firing squad, and shot.
> Tsali's family escaped, and they got
> with other stubborn ones into the hills
> and hid, and to this day Cherokees still,
> descended from those hardy ones, remain
> in the eastern hills.

My father's father was known as Major Ridge, and this is how he came to have that name. Major Ridge was the older of two brothers. He was first known as Nung-noh-hut-tah-hee, or the Pathkiller, and his brother was Oo-watie, the Ancient One. As he grew older, my grandfather was often heard to reply, when asked whence he came, "I came along the top of the mountain." This reply, shortened and put into English, became his name. And he became the Ridge.

When the Cherokees went to war against the whites in 1788 because of the murder of our great Chief Old Tassel, my Grandfather Ridge was one of the foremost warriors, though he was but seventeen years of age. I wish I could have seen him in those days—head shaved, scalp lock tied with red and white feathers, face painted, and clad only in moccasins and breechclout. I know that he presented a formidable figure to his enemies. And in the wars that followed, he did his part. These wars were ended by negotiations in Philadelphia with George Washington in 1794. During the relatively peaceful years that followed, Grandfather Ridge became a prominent Cherokee councilman, due in part to his tremendous oratorical skills. It was also during this time that he married the woman who became my grandmother, Sehoya, whose English name was Susanna Wicket.

During this time, due partly to the influence of our Indian agent, Benjamin Hawkins, but largely because of the conviction held by certain Cherokees that doing so would allow us to remain peacefully in our ancient homelands, many Cherokees began to adapt to the ways of the white man. My grandmother became a spinner and a weaver. Grandfather Ridge built a large house like a white man's, cleared his fields, grew cotton, and raised horses, cattle and hogs. I still can almost see the extensive fields of cotton and corn and the beautiful apple and peach orchards he maintained. It was in this setting that my father, John Ridge, the second of five children, was born, in the year 1803.

Another important event in the life of the Ridge, and one that carried ominous overtones, occurred in 1807. A prominent Cherokee named Doublehead accepted bribes from the U.S. secretary of war and negotiated away by treaty vast acres of our best lands. This was not the first time Doublehead had betrayed his people, but it was to be the last, for our leaders determined to put an end to his chicanery. Alexander Saunders, James Vann, and Grandfather Ridge were selected to execute Doublehead for his crimes against the people. On the way to fulfill their sacred obligation, Vann became ill, but my grandfather and Saunders went ahead. In Hiwasee, at a tavern, they waited for Doublehead. The wretch was already drunk when he arrived at the tavern and sat down at the table. Saunders thrust a candle in front of Doublehead's face. Grandfather, having got a good look at Doublehead, rushed over, blew out the candle, and fired his pistol into the side of the traitor's head just below the ear. Grandfather and Saunders then left the tavern, thinking they had accomplished their task, but soon they heard that the bullet had passed through Doublehead's jaw and not killed him. The wounded man had been taken to the loft at the home of a man named Black. Saunders and Grandfather recruited two additional men to accompany them, and the four of them broke into Mr. Black's loft. Grandfather and Saunders aimed pistols simultaneously at Doublehead and pulled the triggers, but both pistols misfired. Doublehead, wounded though he was, sprang from his bed, but his heels caught in the sheets. As he fell forward, he clutched at Grandfather Ridge, and the two of them engaged in desperate hand-to-hand combat. Saunders reprimed his pistol, while the two other men merely stood by observing. Saunders fired a shot, which went through Doublehead's hips, and the struggle continued. Then Saunders pulled out his war axe and drove it with all his might into Doublehead's skull. The old chief at last collapsed on the floor.

For nearly a decade and a half following this incident, all the most strenuous efforts of my grandfather were directed at preserving the homelands of our people. At the suggestion of President Jefferson, the Council of the Cherokee Nation determined to develop a set of written laws, and to this end they appointed a national committee of thirteen. The Ridge was one of that number.

When General Andrew Jackson moved his army against the Red Stick Creeks, the Ridge, with many other Cherokees, including the adopted Cherokee Sam Houston, joined the U.S. Army as volunteers. It was during this action against the Creeks that Grandfather achieved the rank he adopted as part of his name and became Major Ridge.

My grandfather's brother, Oowatie, had also by this time Anglicized his name and was known as Stand Watie. Uncle Stand had a son whom he named Buck. Buck Watie and his cousin, my father, were about the same age, and their fathers, being convinced that the path to success for the Cherokees was the white man's way, sent them both away to school. They both returned home well educated and with white wives. Uncle Buck also came home with a new name. He was calling himself Elias Boudinot. For several years these four men were the strongest voices on behalf of our people in the struggle against the government of Georgia and the U.S. government's removal policy. However, they came to believe that the struggle was hopeless, and that further resistance would only make the suffering of our people more intense. They began to counsel our people to accept the inevitable, but they were much misunderstood, and they were strongly opposed by Principal Chief John Ross. Finally, the four men signed the treaty that Jackson wanted, and my grandfather, upon signing, said, "I feel as if I had just signed my own death warrant." No doubt he recalled at that time what he had helped to do to Doublehead for the crime of selling tribal lands. Soon after that we moved west and joined the Old Settlers.

Chief Ross and his followers remained behind, refusing to acknowledge the validity of the treaty. Later when President Jackson's patience ran out, they were rounded up like cattle, held in pens, and forcibly removed from the old lands to the west. Many of them died, and the survivors blamed the treaty signers as much as they did the United States.

Father had been extremely ill with fever, chest pains, and violent coughing fits, and, at his own insistence, Mother had made him a bed in the living room. I was sound asleep in my own bed the awful night that Father met his end. But it was not the sickness that killed him. It was the far greater sickness of our Nation. I was but twelve years old at the time.

I remember hearing the sound of many horses riding up the road to our house, but I did not quite come out of my slumber until I heard a loud crash, the sound of someone smashing in our door. I saw my mother run past me to the door that led to the room where Father was sleeping. When she reached the doorway, I saw her stopped abruptly by the rough, dark hands of a stranger. She screamed. I jumped out of bed and ran to her side. Mother grabbed me with both her hands and tried to hold me behind her to shield from me the awful spectacle in the next room. But I saw.

I saw a crowd of men with guns and knives. I saw two men dragging my father across the room. Each had him by one of his arms, and they thrust him viciously against the wall. No sooner had they done that than another man

28

stepped forward and plunged a knife deep into my father's chest.

"Stop it," I shouted.

Mother screamed and held me more tightly. Then another knife flashed, and another. Blood splattered across the room. I do not know how many men were in the room or how many of them stabbed and slashed my father as he was held helpless against the wall. It seemed an eternity to me, and it seemed as if the blood would never stop. Finally, the men ran back outside, dragging Father with them. I jerked desperately and tore myself loose from my mother's grasp.

She shouted my name, but I kept running until I had reached the front door. There I stopped in horror. I saw my father flying up into the air. They had apparently tossed him with all their might. He fell back to the ground and landed with an awful thud. Screaming and shouting, the assassins ran one at a time and stamped on his helpless body as they made their way back to their horses to make good their escape.

My mother shoved me aside as she ran through the door and rushed to my father's side. I ran after her. She fell to her knees as she reached him, and she gathered his bloody head in her arms.

"John. John."

I saw him try to answer her, but the only sound he could make was a ghastly gurgling noise as blood bubbled out from between his lips. At last I was overcome, and I covered my eyes and ran crying into the woods.

I remember the terrifying events of that awful night as clearly as if they had occurred only yesterday, for night after night, year after year, I have been forced to relive them in vivid, chilling nightmares.

We later discovered that at about the same time my father had been murdered, Uncle Elias had been chopped in the head with a hatchet, and Grandfather Ridge had been shot from his horse in an ambush. It became apparent to us all that the Ross people intended to murder everyone who had signed the treaty on that fateful December day at New Echota. And not only the signers but their friends and political associates—even their families—were in danger. It had long been rumored that the Ross people planned to slaughter all of the male Starrs. They had killed James, Sr., who had been one of the signers, but his son, Tom, had escaped, and Tom Starr was engaged in massive retaliation. The Cherokee Nation rapidly became embroiled in a bloody civil war. My mother took me to Arkansas to safety and from there sent me north to school. I did not like the north and did not like the school. Perhaps under different circumstances I would have, but I was having recurrent nightmares about my father's death, and I was consumed with an overwhelming desire for revenge. I longed to be with Tom Starr, killing the Ross people to avenge my father's death. I wrote to my mother that the climate disagreed with me and that I was constantly ill. She finally gave in to my pleas and allowed me to return to Arkansas. I finished school in Arkansas. All the while I burned with a secret hatred and a bitter desire for revenge. I grew sullen and morose. I did not play with other children. I sulked by myself, read tales of high adventure, and imagined myself engaged in deadly combat with my enemies.

I was not yet twenty years old when I had my one and only chance to live out my fantasies. I was at a dance in Fayetteville when one of the Ross men showed up and, upon discovering my identity, began to taunt me. I soon discovered his political affiliations, called him some filthy names in turn, and challenged him to fight with me outside. No sooner had we rounded the corner behind the big dance barn than he grabbed me by the collar with both hands. Nothing was further from my mind than the notion of a fair fight, and as he pulled me toward him by my collar, I drew my long "Arkansas toothpick" from inside my jacket and sliced his belly open from one side to the other. I stood over him, watched the lifeblood flow out of him, and listened to his death rattles. I exalted in my triumph—and never once have I felt the slightest twinge of regret for this deed. To avoid prosecution and retaliation from his friends and relatives, however, I left the state of Arkansas and relocated to Springfield, Missouri.

But I had tasted the blood of my enemies, and I thirsted for more. I decided, though, that the blood of minions was not enough. I thirsted for the blood of John Ross himself. At that time John Ross symbolized to me all that was evil in the Cherokee Nation. I devised a scheme to form a small army to invade the Cherokee Nation from Missouri and capture and kill John Ross, but for my plan to succeed, I needed help from within the Cherokee country—and some good military advice. I therefore attempted to enlist the aid of my kinsman Stand Watie, but he refused to involve himself in my effort. Nothing came of it. I spent my time in Missouri scheming and dreaming and accomplishing nothing, and so when a party of local residents announced their intentions of emigrating to California in search of gold, I joined them. That was in 1850, and from that date until this, I have lived my life as an expatriate.

The events of my life in California are of little moment, so I will spend little time and effort outlining them here. I did put forth some small efforts in the goldfields but shortly determined that to be a waste. I decided to expend my efforts in another direction and began seeking and finding small writing jobs with various newspapers around the state. I soon managed to make a living for myself with my pen. When the United States Civil War broke out, I found myself viewing that disaster as another opportunity to attack John Ross and his government. Ross was for the Union initially, and Stand Watie had formed a regiment of Cherokee Confederates. My plots in this direction, however, amounted to nothing more than those I had hatched in Missouri.

While I was writing for a living in California, a remarkable thing took place. There were bandits all around the state, many of them Mexican, and each of the Mexican bandits was referred to as "Joaquín." I found myself fascinated by these Joaquíns. From time to time I even imagined myself to be Joaquín. California had once belonged to Mexico, and the Mexicans were, after all, American Indians. Their land had been invaded by the ever-greedy whites. The story was the same. There was no way to escape it. And while I was writing poems and stories for the amusement of the conquering whites, and while my father's murderers were going unpunished, and while my own beloved Cherokee Nation was in the grip of corrupt politicians, these Joaquíns were killing and robbing and raping the whites. I was envious of them. In my mind all the Joaquíns became one, and the one became a great symbol of a kind of brown-skinned avenging angel. I conceived the character and wrote the book *The Life and Adventures of Joaquín Murieta*, and all the while I was engaged in this task, I was vicariously living the action. The white men of California were, in my mind, John Ross, Andrew Jackson, Wilson Lumpkin, and all the red-necks of Georgia and the Ross men of the Cherokee Nation. With my imagination and my pen I did the things that I could not, or would not, do in real life but that I felt I should be doing. *Joaquín Murieta* was, for a time, my salvation.

But only for a time. When I had been away from the Cherokee Nation for several years, and when I had finished my work on *Joaquín Murieta*, I found myself with time to reflect on the past, to analyze events, and to sort out my thoughts. And I realized that by hating the Ross people, I was hating most of my own people. I tried to tell myself that they were ignorant, that they were pawns of Chief John Ross. If I could believe that, then I could focus all my hatred on John Ross, who, after all, was seven-eighths *yoneg*. John Ross, I told myself, was the murderer of my father and my kinsmen. Then I recalled my Grandfather Ridge's fateful words as he signed the Treaty of New Echota. I recalled his part in the execution of Doublehead. I wondered if Doublehead had left a son and a grandson, and, if so, if they were today, like me, longing for revenge. If my grandfather was justified in slaying Doublehead, then would the Ross men not be justified in slaying my grandfather and the others? It was logical, but my emotions would not allow me to accept it. Still, the thoughts plagued my mind. Again I became morose and sullen. My poor wife—ah, I have but mentioned my wife, but perhaps that is for the best. I pray that when I am gone, she will be able to put me out of her mind and begin her life anew. She began to worry about me. She asked what was troubling me, but I could not tell her. She, being white, would never understand. My mind was all confusion. My soul was ill at ease.

I was sick at heart. My country had been devastated. My people were being persecuted. They had been ripped asunder and were sniping at each other, and although it seemed to me that they were in their death throes, I could not even return to my homeland to suffer with them. They suffered there—I here. I was sick. I suffered alone. I suffered not for myself alone but for my people. I no longer found any joy in life. The malaise that had infected me was beginning to create physical symptoms. I was sick at heart and sick in my body. I was plagued by almost constant headaches. My wife endured with me, and because of her suffering, I began to wish that my life would end.

But worst of all were the dreams I had been having and the thoughts those dreams created which plagued my waking hours. Rare was the night when, in my troubled sleep, I was not visited by the old Conjurer. He would walk into my room; I would awaken and sit upright in my bed. I would sweat as if I had run long in the hot sun of my home in the Cherokee Nation. My heart would pound and my eyes, open wide, would not blink; they would burn. The Conjurer would stand just inside my room. He wore buckskin leggings and mocassins decorated with porcupine quills. His long shirt was of buckskin, and he wore an old-fashioned headdress on his shaven head. His face was tattooed and his ears were slit and decorated. He was flanked by two huge, ferocious-looking, black wolves, their lips curled tight in a snarl, saliva dripping from their mouths. After what seemed an interminable silence, his black eyes all the while boring into me, I would find my voice.

"What do you want?" I would ask, my voice trembling, and though I spoke in English, he would answer in Cherokee.

"Burn your big houses," he would say. "Throw away your guns and your steel knives and pots. Kill your cats. Destroy everything you have that came from the white man."

"But why?" I would ask, still speaking in English, and he would answer, again in Cherokee.

"If you forget the ways of your fathers and your fathers' fathers and become like the white man, soon there will be no Cherokees. You are bringing destruction to our people."

"You are a superstitious old fool," I would shout in English, and suddenly I would no longer be myself. I would have become my Grandfather Ridge, and I would be standing on my bed and waving my arms as if I were delivering a public oration.

"Our path to salvation," I would shout, "is the white man's education. It is the only way."

"You are doomed," the Conjurer would say in Cherokee, and his old, bony finger would point at me. "If you do not heed my warning, you will be driven westward until you reach the edge of our world and the great sea. There will be no place left to go."

Suddenly there would be Thunder and Lightning. The wind would begin to blow and rain would fall, and before me I would see the wagons, the horses, the soldiers, and the people—hundreds and hundreds of Cherokee people—walking along the trail to the west. Many would be lying dead beside the trail, and as I watched, others would fall by the wayside. There would be more Thunder and Lightning. Then, as suddenly as before, the sky would be clear and blue, and I would look up at it and around me and find myself alone. I would look down and discover

34

that I was standing barefoot in hot sand, and as I raised my eyes to look ahead, I would discover that I was standing on the California beach with nothing before me but the vast and endless ocean. I would scream and awake, sitting up in my bed, covered with sweat. I wonder—was it a dream? This morning I believe there were grains of sand between my sheets where my feet had been.

Was my grandfather wrong? Were he and my father and the rest of their kind to blame for the suffering of all of my people? Were they at fault? If they had killed their cats and done the other things the old Conjurer told them to do, if they had remained true to the ways of their fathers, would all be well for the Cherokees today? Would we be at home in Georgia and Tennessee raising our children in peace and harmony? I do not know. I have never known life untouched by the white man. All the food I have eaten all my life has been cooked in steel pots. I do not know, but the dream frightened me.

I was afraid, and my headaches continued. Last night my dream was different. I did not scream on the beach and wake up. Instead, as I stood there, the Lightning flashed once more, and I beheld a tremendous rattlesnake. He was coiled, his head was erect, his tail was rattling, his tongue was flickering, and his eyes were fixed on me. I believed that I was looking at the Grandfather of all the rattlesnakes that ever lived.

Today I recalled a story that the old ones used to tell. I have not heard it told for many years. One day, the story goes, a hunter was out in the woods. Suddenly he found himself surrounded by rattlesnakes. There was no way he could turn. As he stood there trying to decide what to do, one very large rattlesnake came forward and raised itself up to speak.

"Just now," said the rattlesnake, "your wife has killed my brother by your house. When you go home, send your wife outside to fetch fresh water. I will be waiting for her there to get revenge for the life of my brother. If you do not agree to this, we will kill you here and now."

35

The hunter agreed, and he went home and did as he had promised. He sent his wife outside, and she was killed by the rattlesnake.

down from a world on top of the sky
down to a world of water
to a world where beetle brought mud
from somewhere beneath the waves
and spread it on top to dry
and be hurried along in the drying
by buzzard's flapping great wings,
the first of the Cherokees came.

In my lifetime I have been thoroughly indoctrinated by the missionaries with the story of Adam and Eve (Red Clay and First Woman). I have been taught to believe that the stories my people have told for centuries are childish superstition and prattle. But lately, here on the western edge of my world, dreams and visitations have been hammering the old prophecies back into my head. The world that the missionaries built in my mind has been crumbling. I have been forced to think about these things. I do not know. I do not know. The missionaries' stories sound to me like fables. I cannot conceive of the notion that my Grandfather Ridge or the old man who now haunts my sleep descended from Adam and Eve. But that the Ridge and the old Conjurer, with his two black beasts, are children of those first men and women who came down from the world on top of the sky seems as natural to me as my own skin.

I got up from bed this morning and did not dress, for I expected to be back in bed before long. I went to my closet and found my rifle. I checked it and started for my yard. Just as I put my hand on the door, something stopped me. I went through the house to the back door and went outside. Out in the yard, I took my rifle by the barrel, and swinging it round my head let it fly as far as I could fling it. I went back in. In the bedroom I found my wife still fast asleep.

"Thank God," I said to myself. "How could I begin to explain to her?"

I went to the closet in the hall, removed a few things that were in my way, and then brought down from the top shelf a long bundle, which I carefully unwrapped. It was my old bow. I strung it and tested the string. It was good. From the same bundle I removed an arrow. I sighted and found it straight. Then, taking the bow and the arrow, I went outside again, this time through the front door. I had taken but four steps away from my porch when I saw it. It was not as big, certainly, as the one in my dream, but it was huge, and it was poised in exactly the same way. We looked at one another for a moment, then I nocked the arrow, pulled the string, and sighted. The great snake rose higher and his mouth opened wider and I let fly the arrow straight into his gaping maw.

I returned to bed and lay down and immediately felt all my strength leave my body. My fear and my headache left with my strength. Now I am quite at peace. My dear wife is very much concerned and is constantly attending to me. I think she will not be required to do so much longer.

The Immortals

"Lieutenant Gatewood?"

"Yes, Sir."

The young lieutenant pitched the dregs from his tin coffee cup, dropped the cup to the ground beside the fire, and rushed over to the major's tent to find out what his commanding officer wanted.

"Come inside, Lieutenant."

"Yes, Sir."

The lieutenant followed the major inside the large command tent. There was a table set up in the middle of the tent. On the table a lamp was burning and a map was spread out.

"I want the troops ready to move out at the crack of dawn," said the major, and he pointed to the map. "We're supposed to be here in two days. We'll have to travel fast, and those two days will be long days. In addition, we have to be prepared to be able to spare the time we might lose should we encounter the enemy."

"Do you expect us to come across any Johnny Rebs, Sir?" asked the lieutenant.

"According to our reports, the only chance we have along this route of coming across any of them will be right here."

Again the major pointed to the map.

"Why, that's just about half the distance we have to

cover, Sir," said the lieutenant. "We should be there about this time tomorrow night."

"Right."

"Will we attack them at night?"

"My orders are to report to General Sherman in two days. If we encounter a large enemy force, we'll have to try to make our way around them unobserved. However, if it's a small force, we'll take them. My sources have informed me that the hill is likely to be occupied by Colonel Thomas and his ragtag band of Cherokee Indians. You can tell the men to be prepared for a skirmish tomorrow night."

"Yes, Sir," said the lieutenant, and the troops moved out early the following morning.

That evening and miles down the road on a hilltop in Tennessee, Tobacco Smoke's Uncle sat behind a makeshift bunker. His rifle was leaning against the rocks beside him as he reached into his pocket for a small stone pipe. He drew out a tobacco pouch and filled the pipe. The sun was just disappearing behind the trees. As Tobacco Smoke's Uncle lit his pipe, a short white man in a Confederate officer's uniform walked up behind him.

"'Siyo, Wil-usdi," said Tobacco Smoke's Uncle.

"Now," said the short man, "how did you know it was me?"

"You don't walk like an Indian, Wil-usdi, and you're the only gu-le behind me. If the Yankees were back there, I'd hear all kinds of noise."

"You Cherokees will never make soldiers," said the white man. "Fighters, maybe, but not soldiers. You know, you should call me Colonel Thomas while we are in the army. Instead, you call me Little Will."

"Sit down and smoke with me, Wil-usdi," said the Cherokee. "Even you make too tall a target standing up on top of a hill if the Yankees come by."

Wil-usdi sat down and took the pipe.

"Tell me," he said as he puffed, "are those old burial mounds I see over there?"

Little Will passed the pipe back to Tobacco Smoke's Uncle, who took it and drew deeply.

"Wil-usdi," he said, "Cherokees used to be all over this part of the country. Now, since the Trail of Tears took most of them away to the west, we few who live by your good will on your land are all that is left here. But one time we were many, many.

"Those are our mounds. Once there was a town right here where we are, and this place out here is called Dayulsunyi, the Place Where They Cried. That's because of the Immortals."

"The Immortals?" said Little Will. "I thought I'd heard all of your tales, but I don't recall any Immortals."

Tobacco Smoke's Uncle puffed his pipe.

"Once, before you gu-les came," he said, "a large army of Indians came into our country. No one knew who they were or where they came from. They attacked the Lower Towns and killed many Cherokees. They burned our towns. They were coming this way to attack the very town that used to be right here."

"Here," said Little Will, "where we are camped?"

"Right here. And the Cherokees knew they were coming, and they got ready to fight. They knew that the strangers were many and strong, but they meant to defend their town. So they sent some scouts out there in the woods to watch."

Tobacco Smoke's Uncle gestured toward the woods in front of the hill on which they sat. He puffed on his pipe a few times before resuming his story.

"Pretty soon those scouts came back and said the strangers were coming. There were many more of them than of the Cherokees, and the Cherokee men and even some women got their weapons and waited for the enemy to attack. But some of them wanted to run and hide, because the attackers were so many. An argument broke out, and pretty soon, while the Cherokees were still arguing, here came the attackers, right out of those woods. Some of

40

the Cherokees were about to run, when a man, or something that looked like a man, came walking right out of the side of one of those mounds over there that you were asking about. He was dressed like a Cherokee, and he was ready for war. He waved his war club in the air, and he called out to the Cherokees to stand and fight. Then another came out behind him, and more and more until there were hundreds of them, and they led the attack against the invaders.

"The enemy was surprised to see so many Cherokees there, but they were brave men and good fighters, so they got ready for a big fight, but then the Immortals became invisible to the enemy. The enemy couldn't see them. All they could see was war clubs floating in the air and hundreds of arrows flying. The Cherokees followed the invisible ones, and with their help they whipped the invaders real bad. They killed most of them, and the ones they didn't kill sat down and cried and begged the Cherokees not to kill them. Then the chief of the Immortals, the one who had come out of the mound first, told the Cherokees to let those few remain alive so they could go back to where they came from and tell their people what had happened to them here. Then the Immortals went back inside their mounds."

Tobacco Smoke's Uncle handed his pipe to Little Will. The white man took the pipe, and he leaned back against the rocks as he puffed it.

"Hm-mm-m," he murmured.

Not far away, through the woods in front of the hill, the Yankee major had halted his troops and sent Lieutenant Gatewood and a sergeant to scout ahead. He had dismounted and was pacing back and forth beneath a tree when Gatewood returned.

"Well, Lieutenant?" he said. "What did you find? Is it Colonel Thomas and his Indians?"

"I don't know about that, Sir," said Gatewood, "but there's hundreds of them up there."

41

"What?"

"Hundreds."

"My intelligence sources assured me that Thomas had no more than two dozen or so Indians left with him."

"Well, I don't know who's up there, Sir, but whoever it is, they're all over those hills."

"Lieutenant," said the major, "turn the column and find a way around the rebels. Instruct the men to remain absolutely silent until we get around this."

"Yes, Sir," said the lieutenant, and he hurried away to carry out his orders.

On the hilltop ahead, Wil-usdi having gone back to the campsite to his bedroll, Tobacco Smoke's Uncle sat alone on watch, puffing his pipe.

Wili Woyi

Wili Woyi sat in the small clearing behind his cabin. The great rocks rose sharply just behind the clearing, and above and behind the rocks lay the hills, covered with woods. In the small clearing, Wili Woyi sat, and he burned tobacco—*tsola gayunli*. And as the smoke from the burning *tsola gayunli* rose upward toward the rocks, toward the hills, toward the clouds rolling overhead, Wili Woyi repeated, in Cherokee, seven times, the following charm.

> Listen.
> They will speak well of me today
> there at Illinois.
> Those who would do me harm
> will be wandering about.
> Today I will ride back home again.
> Ha.

Later that same morning Wili Woyi rode toward the Illinois Courthouse in the Illinois District of the Cherokee Nation, where he was to stand trial for having killed a man. He was going in alone. He had given his word that he would appear, and his word had been accepted. He was known as a man of honor. Wili Woyi was a man of honor, but he also knew that he had nothing to fear, for the killing had been in self-defense and, as such, was provided for in the Cherokee National Constitution. Wili Woyi knew that the Cherokee courts were fair, and he knew that Benge, the judge for the Illinois District, was a fair, honorable, and intelligent judge. The trial would be brief, and he would soon be on his way back home. He rode with confidence.

Then from ahead he heard the sound of fast hoofbeats. He could not see the rider for the bend in the road, but as he rounded the bend, he recognized his friend Turtle Brashears. When Turtle saw Wili Woyi, he called out to him in Cherokee and reined in his mount.

"Wili Woyi. Wili Woyi. Go back."

Wili Woyi, too, stopped his horse.

"What is it, Turtle? Why should I go back? You know that I have given my word to appear in court today because of that man I killed. I cannot go back now."

"It is because of that man that I ask you to go back, Wili Woyi. You will be hanged if you do not go back."

"I am no murderer, Turtle, and our courts are just. They will not hang me. Come. Ride in with me."

"No. Wait. There will not be a trial. Not today and not in Illinois Courthouse. That is why I have ridden out here to meet you and to stop you from going to court. Judge Benge knows that I have come out here to meet you, though he must keep that a secret."

"Perhaps you should tell me what is going on at Illinois Courthouse, Turtle."

"Yes. There is a United States lawman waiting there to take you to Fort Smith for trial. There is nothing that Benge can do anymore. That man you killed—he was not of our Nation."

"Ha," said Wili Woyi, smacking his hand to his forehead, "then you are right. I will not be taken to Fort Smith to the hanging judge, Parker. It is part of his divine purpose, it seems, to hang Indians in order to bring the law of the yoneg to our country. He would hang me for sure. I will not go in now."

44

"What will you do, Wili Woyi?"

Wili Woyi looked up at the sky.

"Ulogila," he said. "It's cloudy. Come on, Turtle, let's go to my house."

At Illinois Courthouse a crowd had gathered. There were a number of Cherokees standing about, not waiting to see if Wili Woyi would show up, for they knew that once Turtle intercepted him on the road and told him the news, he would not, but to see what the white lawman from Fort Smith would do when he realized that Billy Pigeon was not going to arrive. The white lawman was pacing about nervously in front of Illinois Courthouse. The Cherokees were standing calmly with crossed arms, leaning against the sides of the courthouse, or sitting idly about under the great walnut trees and cottonwoods that stood nearby. Benge stood in the doorway of the courthouse. Then the white lawman, who was called Glenn Colvert, took a watch from his vest-pocket and looked at it.

"He's forty minutes late now, goddamn it. I knew he wouldn't come in here by hisself like you said he would. I never heard of such goddamn foolishness."

"You have no patience, Mr. Colvert," said Benge. "We Cherokees have a different way of looking at time than do you whites. If a Cherokee promises he will be somewhere, then he will be there. He may not be there on time, for we have never lived our lives according to clocks as you do. But Wili Woyi—uh, excuse me, Billy Pigeon is a man of honor."

"Yeah," said Colvert, "so you told me. Look, Benge, ain't you got no deputies here you can send out after him? I can't stand around here all goddamn day. I got other things to do, too, you know."

"The case is out of my hands now, Mr. Colvert. You should know that. The man that Wili Woyi killed was not a Cherokee citizen, and, as you know, your government will not allow our courts jurisdiction over such cases. Otherwise, why should you be here? If Wili Woyi has not broken Cherokee law, how can Cherokee law take any action against him?"

"Damn it, Benge, I know all that, but you know as well as I do that that's just a goddamned technicality. He's killed a man, and I got a legal warrant for his arrest right here in my coat pocket."

"And it's your job to serve that warrant. I have no intention of interfering with you in the line of your duty. Serve the warrant, Mr. Colvert, any time you please. I, however, will not break the laws by arresting a man outside of the jurisdiction of my court."

"Aw, son of a bitch."

"Mr. Colvert, I suggest you go inside and try to relax. I believe it's going to rain any minute now. I'm sure that if you'll just be patient, Wili Woyi will show up, and then you can arrest him."

"You people think you're pretty goddamned smart, don't you? You think you've made a fool out of a duly appointed officer of the law of the United States government. Well, it ain't going to work. I can tell you that. Maybe I ain't got Bill Pigeon right now. Maybe I ain't even going to get him today, but I'll be coming back, and I'll get the son of a bitch, and I'll have him at Fort Smith in the court."

Colvert stalked to his horse, which was tied nearby. He jerked the reins loose from the hitching rail, mounted up hurriedly, and started to ride off, but an afterthought made him turn back to shout over his shoulder to Benge and all the other Cherokees within hearing.

"And I'll see to it personal that you all get a invitation to the hanging."

When Wili Woyi and Turtle Brashears arrived at the cabin below the great rocks, they took the saddles from their horses' backs and turned the animals out to graze. Wili Woyi invited Turtle into his house.

"Danatlasdayunni. We will eat," he said.

He poured coffee grounds into a pot, picked up a heavy

iron skillet, and handed pot and skillet to Turtle. He found half a cake of cornbread left from earlier in another pot, and, taking it up, he led the way back outside and around behind his cabin. There he built a small fire, filled the coffee pot with water from a bucket, and set it on to boil. He walked to the small smokehouse he had built up against the great rocks and returned with several medium-sized perch, already cleaned, and put them in the skillet to fry.

"Ha," said Turtle, "are these the largest you could catch in the Illinois?"

"I caught one very large," said Wili Woyi, "this long," and he held his hands apart so far that Turtle raised his brows.

"It was the first one," said Wili Woyi.

Turtle chuckled. He knew that Wili Woyi, according to tradition, always threw back into the water the first fish he caught, no matter what the size, and upon throwing it back, said to the fish, "It was the fishinghawk." This, of course, was a ruse intended to misdirect any vengeful spirits who might seek restitution for violence done to the fish by sending into the body of the fisherman some dread disease.

Later, fish fried and eaten, coffee drunk, the two friends settled back. Now is the time for talk—after eating. Turtle stared up at the gray clouds.

"This thing is not over, Wili Woyi," he said.

"No," answered the other, "it will not be over. With Parker's men after me, it will not be over."

"What will you do?"

Wili Woyi had been rolling cigarettes. He finished, handed one to Turtle, picked a faggot with a glowing end from the fire, and held it out while Turtle lit his smoke. Then he lit his own. He leaned back again on one elbow, drawing deeply on the cigarette.

"I will live, Turtle," he said finally. "What should I do? As usual, I will live my life. These men from Parker—they must simply become a part of my life."

Wili Woyi felt the first few drops of rain fall against his cheek.

"Agasga," he said. "It's raining."

They gathered up the pots and went back inside the cabin.

Horse Jackson had a bad pain in his stomach. He had had it for three days. On the morning of the fourth day of his misery he awoke still in pain. As he moaned audibly, his wife, Quatie, said, "Your insides still hurt you?"

"Ahhh," Horse groaned, "yes, as much as ever."

"Some angry spirit has gotten inside you because of something you've done—or have neglected to do," said Quatie, who was a good Baptist, as was her husband, but who saw no reason why the spirits should not attack Baptists as well as anyone else.

"Ah," said Horse, "it is three days now."

"Today will be four," answered his wife. "Four is a good day. Go to Wili Woyi. If anyone can find the cause of your pain and drive it away, Wili Woyi can."

"Perhaps you are right. There is no wiser *didahnuwisgi*, no wiser man of medicine, in our Nation than Wili Woyi. He has more charms than anyone else. But what can I give him? We have no money."

"Take these tobacco seeds," said Quatie. "I was saving them for our own use, but what good will even this good Georgia tobacco do us when you are ill if we do not know the charms with which to use it? Take the seeds."

Deputy Marshal Glenn Colvert squinted his eyes through the rain and through the stream that was running off the brim of his hat. There before him was what, according to directions he had been given, should be the house of Bill Pigeon. The sharp rise of the hills behind the cabin would make a quick escape to the rear, if not impossible, at least difficult and improbable.

"That's good," thought Colvert, "first damn thing all day, but that's good."

48

He climbed, creaking, down out of his saddle and looped the reins of his mount twice quickly around the trunk of a nearby bois d'arc sapling. He removed the rifle from the saddleboot and started slowly for the cabin, keeping well in under the trees. His boots squished with each step.

"Goddamn rain," he thought.

Inside the cabin, Wili Woyi and Turtle Brashears drank coffee and smoked the cigarettes Wili Woyi had rolled.

"It is a good rain," Turtle was saying. "It will be good for my corn."

"And for everything else," added Wili Woyi. "It was much needed."

Outside, Colvert cranked a shell into the chamber of his rifle. He aimed above Wili Woyi's house, fired, and quickly refilled the chamber. Then he yelled at the top of his lungs, "Pigeon. Bill Pigeon."

Wili Woyi was up, rifle in hand, at his front window in an instant, and Turtle was not much slower. He, too, had a rifle.

"Pigeon."

"Who's that?" shouted Wili Woyi in English. "Who are you?"

"This here's Deputy United States Marshal Glenn Colvert, Pigeon, and I've got a warrant for your arrest right here in my coat pocket. Now, I don't want no trouble from you. I don't want to kill nobody if I don't have to. My orders is to take you in for trial."

Turtle asked Wili Woyi, "How many with him, do you think?"

"I do not know, Turtle. He is alone, I think. I am not sure."

"We two can kill him."

"No, Turtle. Then there would be warrants for two."

"We can go out the back way, into the hills."

"And maybe then we would get shot in our backs, too."

Colvert called again, "Pigeon. What do you say?"

Wili Woyi turned to Turtle.

"Turtle, the time is not right to fight or to run. Later will be the right time, maybe. Right now I will go with this deputy. Take my rifle and do not show your face. I do not think he knows that anyone is with me."

Turtle Brashears took the rifle. He did not say anything.

"Deputy," called Wili Woyi, "I am coming out. I will go with you."

"No goddamn guns. No funny stuff," said Colvert.

"No guns, Deputy."

Wili Woyi kicked open the front door of his cabin and walked out into the rain, hands held high.

Deputy Marshal Colvert made Wili Woyi saddle his own horse at gunpoint, then he put handcuffs on him and told him to mount up. He tied the Indian's feet together underneath the belly of the horse and led them to the bois d'arc to which he had tied his own mount, then they headed toward Muskogee and the nearest railroad depot. Wili Woyi had not spoken a word since coming outside. They rode most of the rest of that day—as long as there was light, but because of the heavy rain the light did not last as long that day as was usual for a summer day. On the west bank of the Grand River, Colvert ordered Wili Woyi to stop at the mouth of a small cave. There was enough overhanging rock above to give the horses some shelter. Colvert staked them out, untied Wili Woyi's feet and allowed him to dismount, then tied them again and prepared a camp for the night. He built a small fire, made some coffee, and heated a can of beans. Wili Woyi refused the beans but accepted a cup of the hot coffee. Still, he did not speak.

When Colvert had finished his beans and coffee, he unlocked the cuffs from one of Wili Woyi's wrists and locked them again with the Indian's hands behind his back. He checked the ropes binding his prisoner's feet together. Satisfied, he tossed a blanket over Wili Woyi, then, with a loud fart, crawled into his own bedroll. Soon he was sleeping peacefully. Wili Woyi was still awake, still sitting upright. It was not yet quite dark. It was no longer light. It was the second best time of day for speaking to the spirits, the best time of all being the similar time between dark and light in the morning. Wili Woyi turned his eyes toward the clouds. He spoke out loud, but in a very low voice. He spoke, in Cherokee, the following words:

> Hey.
> You spirits on high—
> You *anidawe*—
> you who dwell
> in *umwadahi*—
> come down at once.
> Get into the brain of that man—
> that man who thinks evil of me.
> Hey.
> Instantly you have come down.
> You have gone into that man.
> He will not hear me.
> He will not see me.
> He will not even awaken
> until well past dawn.
> Hey.
> You *anidawe*
> who dwell on high,
> I will escape from that man.
> *Yu.*

Wili Woyi spat four times toward the sleeping Colvert and repeated the charm four times, spitting again at the end of each recitation. By the time he had finished his ritual, total darkness had set in, and the hard rain had diminished to a light but steady drizzle.

While the heavy rain was still falling, before the light of day had fully disappeared, Turtle Brashears still sat in the house of Wili Woyi, pondering what to do, when he heard the sound of an approaching wagon. The events of the day had made Turtle a bit jumpy, and he ran to the window with his rifle in hand. As he looked out into the rain, he recognized the wife of Horse Jackson sitting in the driver's seat. He put down the rifle and ran out into the rain.

"Quatie, osiyo," said Turtle.

Then he saw that Horse Jackson was lying in the bed of the wagon wrapped up in blankets, the hard rain pouring over him. Horse did not speak. He did not even show any sign that he had seen or heard Turtle.

"We must get him inside quickly," said Turtle.

And quickly, he and Quatie Jackson carried the ailing man inside, where they undressed and dried him and wrapped him in dry blankets. They made him a pallet beside Wili Woyi's fireplace, and Turtle built the fire up. Then he went back out into the rain to care for the Jacksons' horses before returning to the fire to make coffee. He and Quatie drank coffee. Then Quatie spoke.

"My husband has been very ill these four days," she said. "We decided that he should come to Wili Woyi and bring tobacco. Then he became worse and could not even drive, so I had to bring him here."

"Ah," replied Turtle, "Wili Woyi is not here. I do not know when he will return. You know, he killed that man a while back, and there was to be a trial today at Illinois Courthouse with Judge Benge. Wili Woyi was not worried, as that man needed killing, and Benge is a fair judge. But then they discovered that the man was not of our Nation, and so the trial could not be held at Illinois Courthouse. A lawman came from Fort Smith, and he arrested Wili Woyi today. I wanted to kill the lawman, but Wili Woyi would not let me. He said it was not the time."

Turtle paused.

"I do not know when he will be back."

Quatie stared at the floor.

"I do not know what I should do."

"Wait here," said Turtle. "Wait a little. Perhaps Wili

Woyi will return, and Horse needs to rest and stay dry anyway. Wait here. Wili Woyi will come back maybe."

He poured more coffee.

The sun had been up and the rain had been over for about thirty minutes before Glenn Colvert opened his eyes. He yawned and stretched. He propped himself up on one elbow, hacked and spat, then looked over to where he had left his prisoner. All he could see was his blanket, lying there in a wad. He blinked and rubbed his eyes, then suddenly threw off his cover. He jumped to his feet and started for the blanket. His left foot became tangled in his bedroll, and he dragged it a couple of steps with him before he managed to get it loose. Running in his stocking feet, he reached the blanket and jerked it up from the ground. There were the handcuffs, still locked, and there, too, were the ropes with which he had tied Bill Pigeon's feet, his knots still in them. He picked up the ropes and the cuffs, looking hard at them as if they might tell him something. He looked around at the rocks and the trees. His horse still stood where he had hobbled it, but Bill Pigeon's mount was gone. There were no tracks to be seen, neither human nor animal. The rain had seen to that.

"Goddamn it," he thought, "he could be anywhere out there. He could be long gone or he could be laying for me."

Another thought occurred to Colvert, and he hurriedly checked his weapons. Bill Pigeon had not touched them. Then he was still unarmed, and the chances were that he was as far away as time had allowed him to get. Colvert considered going after him, but he could not decide where to look. Bill Pigeon would surely not return to his cabin so soon after having been arrested there, not with the same man who had arrested him likely to be on his trail. If he was not returning to his home, he might be going in any direction, and with the tracks having been washed away by the rain, Colvert could only guess at a direction in which to look. Pigeon probably had Cherokee friends and relatives all through the hills. He might be anywhere. Colvert thought for a moment, and then forced himself to admit that he had simply lost his prisoner. He picked up the ropes and cuffs once more and looked at them.

"Goddamn it," he thought, "it just ain't possible. There just ain't no way."

The rain was still falling when Wili Woyi rode up to his cabin, and neither Turtle Brashears nor Quatie Jackson heard the sound of the approaching horse. When Wili Woyi walked through the front door, the other two jumped quickly to their feet.

"Wili Woyi," said Turtle, "I am glad to see you back. That lawman . . . ?"

"I left him snoring, Turtle. But what is this? Quatie? Your man is ill?"

"For four days now, Wili Woyi. In his stomach it hurts. And now his head is hot. We have tobacco seeds from Georgia."

"Thank you. The seeds will wait. We do not know if Horse will wait."

Wili Woyi removed his wet hat and coat and knelt beside the sleeping Horse Jackson. He looked long at his patient. He felt the head, the chest, the stomach. He looked at Quatie.

"Four days?"

"Yes."

"How long has he been this way?"

"He was awake when we left our home, but he was in much pain. Sometime on the way here he went to sleep."

Wili Woyi poured himself some coffee from the pot which Turtle had kept fresh and hot and took a long sip. Then he went back to Horse Jackson.

"Horse," he said. "Horse. This is Wili Woyi. Do you hear me?"

"Ahhh," Horse struggled to comprehend.

"Can you tell me how you feel, Horse?"

"Agwesdaneha," said Horse. "I am in pain."

"We will fix it, Horse. It will go away."

When Glenn Colvert stepped off the train the next day at Fort Smith, he headed directly for the office of his immediate superior, U.S. Marshal Moss Berman. Colvert desperately wanted a glass of whiskey, but he knew Berman well enough to know that the drink had better wait until he had made his official report—a report, by the way, that he did not relish making. He had failed, and Moss Berman did not take failure lightly. He, himself, seldom failed to accomplish his purpose, and he expected the same from the men who rode for him—for the law. Colvert took a deep breath and knocked on the door.

"Come on in."

Colvert entered.

"Moss?"

"I heard the train pull in, Glenn. You got your prisoner turned in already?"

"Well, no Moss, . . ."

"Where is he? You have to kill him?"

"No, but, damn it, I should have. Hell, Moss, I ain't got him."

Colvert stood shuffling his shoes on the floor like a teenager waiting for a scolding, but he was waiting instead for an outburst from Moss Berman—an outburst that never came. It would have been easier on the deputy's nerves if it had. Moss Berman took a long, black cigar from his inside coat pocket, bit off an end and spat it out, took his time wetting down the cigar, and finally struck a match on the front of his desk and lit it.

"What happened?" he asked in a quiet voice.

"Well, you know, Moss, that there Pigeon, he was lined up for a trial in the Cherokee courts. He was supposed to show up at that Illinois Courthouse, so that's where I went to fetch him. The Injun judge and a whole mess of Injuns was standing around there waiting for him, and they kept swearing to me that Pigeon would be there, but he never showed. So I went on out to his house, and he was there just bigger than shit, and he never even give me no trouble. I hollered out for him to come on out, that he was under arrest, and he come. I tied him up and we tuck out. Well, come nightfall, I bedded us down. Now, Moss, goddamn it, I know how to hog-tie a prisoner. You know I do. I tied that son of a bitch up good. I tied his feet, and I cuffed his hands. There wasn't no way nobody could have got out of them ropes and irons. Nobody."

"But Bill Pigeon did?"

"Yessir. God bless me, Moss, he did. When I woke up come morning, his horse was gone, and he was, too. Right there where I left the son of a bitch, there on the ground, there was my blanket that I had throwed over him, and under that damn blanket—Moss, this here next is crazy, but I swear, Moss—them cuffs was laying right there still locked, and them ropes was laying right there with my knots still tied in them. Right here they is. I ain't done nothing to them but just bring them along to show you."

Colvert pulled the ropes and the cuffs out of the pocket of his yellow slicker and held them out to Moss Berman. Berman took them, and Colvert continued to stare accusingly at them.

"Well," he went on, "I looked around, but I never seen no sign of no kind. If Pigeon left any, the rain wiped them on out."

Moss Berman tossed the ropes and cuffs back across his desk toward Glenn Colvert and puffed on his cigar.

"Glenn, go on over and get yourself a drink and a good meal and a bath. You need all of them. Then you get yourself a good night's sleep. In the morning, round up Monk and Estey. The three of you are taking the first train out of here for Muskogee tomorrow. That warrant you're carrying is for murder. I want it served, and I want it served now."

Wili Woyi had given him the specially prepared drink and had sung over him, and now Horse Jackson was resting. Quatie watched over him inside the cabin, and Wili Woyi and Turtle Brashears were outside in back of the cabin smoking.

"Wili Woyi," said Turtle, "what will you do about this lawman? I think that you should have killed him. Or you should have let me kill him for you when I wanted to. He did not follow you back here when you escaped from him probably because he did not expect you to be so foolish as to return straightaway to your own home, but he will come back here looking for you one day. Will you kill him then? Perhaps there will be more of them with him that time. It will not be so easy as it would have been before."

"He will come back here again, of course," answered Wili Woyi, "and most likely he will have others with him, but this time I will be prepared for him. There are ways, you know, to protect one's home from intruders."

"So I have heard, but I have never seen it done."

"Nor will you, Turtle. Some kinds of magic must be worked alone or the power will be lost. You know, for instance, that I cannot allow you to look upon my tobacco— that which I have prepared."

"Yes, I know."

"As soon as Horse Jackson is ready to move, I want you to go with them to help Quatie get him home safely. He will be ready soon. When I am alone again, I will prepare my home. I will be ready from now on. The lawmen will not enter my house."

Horse Jackson slept the rest of that morning. At noon Quatie fed him some stew Wili Woyi had prepared. About the middle of the afternoon, the Jacksons, having given the Georgia tobacco seeds to Wili Woyi, left for home accompanied by Turtle Brashears. Wili Woyi undressed and slept. He slept soundly until just before dawn the next morning. Then he arose and went to a corner of his room where he kept a leather pouch. He untied the thongs with which the pouch was bound and withdrew from inside a small handful of tobacco. He was still naked. He did not bother to put on any clothing. It was dawn.

Off to the left side of Wili Woyi's cabin, coming from the rocks behind, ran a small stream. The water in the stream was cold and clear. To the edge of this stream Wili Woyi walked, taking with him tobacco. He faced the east and held the tobacco before him in his left hand. With the four fingers of his right hand he stirred the tobacco in his palm in a counterclockwise motion as he repeated four times the following words.

> Ha.
> From the four directions
> they are bringing their souls.
> Just now
> they are bringing their souls.

After each repetition Wili Woyi blew his breath upon the tobacco, and when he had finished, he held the tobacco up toward the rising sun. He returned to his cabin, wrapped the tobacco in a piece of newspaper, and placed it under the pouch in the corner of the room. Then he dressed and made his morning coffee.

When he had finished a leisurely breakfast and had plenty of coffee, he rolled and smoked a cigarette. Then he went back to the spring where he was keeping a bucket of crawdads. He took a few for bait and disappeared into the woods.

Wili Woyi returned home just in time for sundown. He set aside his catch of fish for later cleaning. Then he took up his pipe. It was only a handmade, corncob pipe, but it was serviceable, and it would do. He retrieved the tobacco that he had prepared that morning, and then, pipe in one hand, tobacco in the other, he went outside and to the east of his house. He filled the bowl of the pipe and lit it. Puffing slowly but steadily, Wili Woyi began to walk around his house. In a counterclockwise direction he walked in a huge circle. He paused to blow smoke toward the north, and again toward the west, the south, and finally the east when he had arrived back at his starting point. This circling he repeated four times, making each circle larger than the last. Then he returned to the cabin to clean his fish, confident that he would not be disturbed in his home for at least six months.

Turtle Brashears was driving the wagon for the Jacksons. Horse was lying in the back, but he was awake and feeling much better. Quatie Jackson rode on the seat beside Turtle.

"Wili Woyi is a marvelous doctor," Horse was saying. "I cannot begin to tell you how much better I feel already. He has much power."

"Indeed he has," answered his wife. "You could not have known, of course, but when we arrived at his house, Wili Woyi was not there. He was carried off by some lawman."

"What?"

"Yes," said Turtle. "I was worried about him, but I shouldn't have been. Wili Woyi escaped from that man, and he did not even have to kill him. His magic is very great."

"This lawman," said Horse, "what was he?"

"He was from Parker," said Turtle. "Recently, as you may know, Wili Woyi was forced to kill a man who was trying to rob him. He reported this killing as any good citizen would do, and there was to be a trial at Illinois Courthouse, but before the trial happened, they discovered at Fort Smith that this man, the thief, was not of our Nation. So a lawman came from Parker to arrest Wili Woyi, and he got him. I was there, and I wanted to kill the lawman. Wili Woyi said that I may not, and he went with him, but, as you know, he came back later. He escaped by magic. He did not need to fight with the fool."

"Turtle," said Horse Jackson, "if Wili Woyi has escaped from a white lawman, there will be more of them. They will not stop looking for him, and since he has made a fool of one of them, they will not be so careful next time just to arrest him. They may kill him. Maybe we should go back there with our guns and help him. Wili Woyi is a great man, and it would not be right to let those dogs from Fort Smith get him."

"I agree with you, Horse," said Turtle, "but Wili Woyi sent me away with you just now. He is working some magic—I think against the lawmen. I think Wili Woyi will not be so easy for them to catch or to kill."

"I have heard that Wili Woyi is not only a great *adahnuwisgi*," said Quatie, "but that he is also a master of *didisgahlidodiyi*."

"Ah, yes," said Turtle, "indeed, he can make himself invisible, and not only that, but if he wishes to, he can put his soul into the body of something else. Sometimes he will go into an owl. I have seen these things."

"Well," said Horse, "perhaps you are right then. Perhaps Wili Woyi will be all right. Perhaps he does not need us."

"Perhaps," added Quatie, "he will be even better off without you."

Glenn Colvert was approaching the home of Wili Woyi for the second time in less than a week, but this time he was not alone. With him rode Harper Monk and Birk Estey, both deputies from Fort Smith assigned by Moss Berman to ride with and assist Colvert in the arrest of Billy Pigeon. Berman considered a man who was wanted for murder and had already escaped once from an experienced deputy to be a serious enough threat to merit additional manpower. It had been a source of embarrassment to Colvert, but as he had lost his prisoner, there was not much he could say. Usually a loud, talkative man, Colvert had been unusually quiet the whole way from Fort Smith to Muskogee by rail and thence on horseback with Monk and Estey.

Just before the point in their journey at which Wili Woyi's cabin would become visible to them, Colvert reined in his mount and called a halt.

"Now, boys," he said, "of course, we ain't got no way of knowing if Pigeon's at home or not, but let's not take no chances. He's sneaky as hell. Believe me. I know. Now, what I suggest we do is I think you two had ought to spread out and go through the woods so one of you comes up on each side of the house. You can cover the back as well as the front that way. I'll give you time to get in position, then I'll move in on the front. I'll call out to him first. Give him a chance to come on out peaceable. But if he takes out the back, you all cut down on him right quick. If he don't come out neither door, then I'll move on in."

It took only a few minutes for Monk and Estey to position themselves, and when Colvert was sure that they had had enough time, he stepped out into the open facing the front of Wili Woyi's cabin, rifle in hand.

"Pigeon," he shouted. "Bill Pigeon."

Then aloud, but only to himself, he muttered, "Seems as how I've been here before."

"Bill Pigeon. You in there?"

The only sounds to answer him were the gentle rustling of the breeze through the giant oaks and walnuts, the scamperings of busy squirrels, the flight of some crows, and, off in the distance, the rapid rat-tat-tat of a woodpecker hard at work. Colvert began moving toward the cabin. Slowly. Cautiously. About half way across the clearing which lay before the cabin, Colvert let his eyes dart rapidly from one side of the cabin to the other. There were no outbuildings in sight. The only place that looked as if it might be used to shelter animals was a depression in the rock behind the cabin and off to Colvert's left. It looked as if it might accommodate two or three horses, but that was about all. It was not too deep, and although it was heavily in shadow, Colvert could see that Wili Woyi's horse was not there. He stopped when he reached the door, paused for an instant, then called out again.

"Pigeon. You in there?"

There was no answer.

Colvert, his heart pounding, tried the door. It opened

easily. He pushed it just a few inches, peering inside. There was dim light inside the cabin.

"Anybody home?"

Still no answer. Colvert shoved the door all the way inside to the wall to be sure that no one was lurking behind it. Then, with one foot across the threshold, he poked his nose inside and slowly looked around. He stepped back outside with a strange and eerie sense of relief.

"Monk. Birk. Come on out, boys. Ain't nobody home. Goddamn it."

As the three riders from Fort Smith disappeared back down the road by which they had come, inside the cabin Wili Woyi uncrossed his legs and rose to his feet. He walked straight across the room to the still open door, leaned with his left hand against the door frame and stared after his departing visitors. With his right hand he raised to his lips the cup of steaming coffee that he held and took a long and satisfying sip.

Glenn Colvert, Monk, and Estey had spent the entire day riding in circles in the woods around Wili Woyi's house—counterclockwise. Colvert thought that Wili Woyi would not have gone far from home, and he was determined that if they searched long and hard enough in the area, they would be certain to find some sign of the fugitive. When darkness fell and they could no longer search effectively, the three deputies began to look for a good campsite. As things worked out, they made their camp in the woods along the bank of the same stream that flowed by Wili Woyi's cabin. They built a fire, made coffee and supper, and ate. When they had finished the coffee and cleaned their dishes in the stream, Colvert told the other two men to get some sleep.

"I'll stay up for a couple of hours and keep watch," he said. "Pigeon might be onto us by now. No sense in being careless. In a couple of hours I'll wake you up, Birk. Then you can watch two hours and wake up Monk. Okay?"

The other two crawled into their bedrolls and were soon asleep. Colvert made more coffee. He built the fire up just a little, for there was a slight chill in the night air. Then he sat down near the fire with a cup of coffee, his rifle across his knees. The two hours dragged slowly by with about the only break in the monotony the eerie hoots of a nearby night owl. When his time had passed, Colvert jostled Birk with his foot.

"Two hours is up, Birk," he said. "You're on."

As Birk yawned, stretched, and moaned, crawling out of the sack, Glenn Colvert laid aside his weapons and pulled off his boots. Soon Colvert was sleeping and Birk was sitting beside the fire with his rifle. Birk yawned and rubbed his eyes. His head fell forward, and he jerked it back upright.

"Shit," he muttered to himself. "Can't fall asleep on watch. Can't do that."

He laid aside his rifle and poured himself a cup of coffee from the pot Colvert had brewed. The owl hooted. Birk jumped.

"Just a hoot owl," he said. "Goddamn hoot owl."

Even having thus reassured himself, Birk found that each time the owl hooted, he jumped. He began to feel that the owl knew that it was startling him and was taking delight in the fact. He thought about trying to locate the villain and shoot it, but immediately he realized that such a course of action would bring Monk and Colvert rapidly to their senses and almost certainly put them in a very bad humor. But the owl hooted again, and Birk jumped again, and he knew that he must do something. He put aside his rifle once more and began to look around on the ground for a stone just the right size. He found and hefted two or three before he settled on one. It was smooth, nearly round, and was quite a fistful. It should do nicely.

Birk stood up slowly with the rock in his right hand and faced in the direction from which the hoots had seemed to come. He strained his eyes into the darkness but could see nothing. Suddenly he heard it again, and he threw the rock with all his might in the direction of the sound. There was a rustling of leaves and the sound of the rock falling to the ground—then silence. Monk snorted and rolled over in his sleep but did not wake up. Colvert showed no sign of having been in the least disturbed. Birk went back to the fire and squatted. He picked up his cup and sipped from it. As he reached to place the cup back on the ground, he stiffened. He heard what he would have sworn to be the sound of footsteps very close by. He reached for his rifle and was astonished when he saw that it was not where he had left it. He drew his revolver, clumsily in his haste, and looked around the camp in all directions. There was no one to be seen. Nothing moved. Poised, ready to shoot, he continued to look. He thought about waking Colvert but did not know what he would tell him. Then he saw his rifle lying beside Colvert's where Colvert slept. He retrieved it.

"I know I left it over here," he muttered, "I know it. I must have moved it over yonder when I was getting after that damned hoot owl. I must have moved it and never knowed it. Too damn jumpy."

He picked up his coffee cup and lifted it to his lips to drink. It was empty.

"Glenn. Glenn," he yelled. "Get up. Monk?"

Glenn Colvert came out first. He had a pistol in each hand. Monk was reaching for his rifle and trying to get his legs out from under his blanket at the same time.

"What is it?" said Colvert.

"Glenn, they's somebody here."

"Where?" said Monk.

"Well, did you see him?"

"No, I never."

"Where'd the sound come from?"

"Right by God here. Right here."

Birk was stamping and pointing to the ground on the other side of the campfire from where he had been sitting.

"Come on, Birk," said Colvert, lowering his guns, "you

mean he was right here behind you, and you never seen him? You been sleeping, Birk?"

"No, Glenn. Damn it, I swear it. I never went to sleep. I was sitting here with a cup of coffee in my hand, and I heard footsteps right here. I looked around and they wasn't nobody there, so I got up to look around some more. Then I seen my rifle was gone. I found it over yonder. Right beside yours. I swear I never put it there. Well, I figured I must be getting spooky, so I went back to the fire, and I found my cup empty, and, Glenn, I hadn't tuck but a sip out of it. I don't know who or what it is, but goddamn it, they's somebody here."

Again Birk stamped the ground around the fire.

"All right, all right," said Colvert. "You go and get some sleep. Monk, you awake? You take on over your watch now. It's a little early, but Birk's too . . . "

Colvert didn't finish what he was saying, for just then there was a loud splashing, followed by a hissing and a clank. All three deputies turned at once and raised their weapons. Their fire was almost out, steam was rising from the ashes, hissing still, and the coffee pot was on its side, rocking a tiny bit in the dirt.

Three Miles Southeast of Illinois Courthouse, Near the Illinois River, Winter, 1891

"Looks like he's been here for some time," one of the men in the group was saying. There were about a dozen of them gathered around to get a good look at the body so recently discovered.

"Yeah," said another. "Hogs or something's been after him. Bet his own mother couldn't recognize him now."

Glenn Colvert shoved his way through the crowd.

"Make some room here, fellows. This here's the law coming through. Make some room."

A path to the body was more or less cleared, and Moss Berman followed Glenn Colvert through it.

"Goddamn," said Colvert, "that's a hell of a sight."

Moss Berman turned and walked away again. He paused a few feet distant under a large walnut tree to light a cigar.

"Reckon who it is?" said one of the men.

"Who it was, you mean," said Colvert.

Berman spoke out in a strong voice.

"It was Bill Pigeon," he said. "I recognize him, even like that."

There were murmurs of surprise and disbelief. Glenn Colvert hurried over to Berman. He spoke in a harsh whisper.

"How can you tell, Moss? I mean, the shape he's in? I had Pigeon under arrest that time, and I can't tell. Fact of the matter is, I don't recall him being as big as this here fellow looks to have been."

Berman sucked at his cigar. Slowly an expression of great puzzlement came over Colvert's face.

"Moss?" he said. "Whenever did you set eyes on Bill Pigeon?"

Berman reached out and took hold of Colvert's necktie. He gave it a gentle tug as if to straighten it. The crowd of spectators was still milling around the body as if they could not get their fill of the gruesome sight—all but one, who seemed more interested in the two lawmen than in the body. Turtle Brashears, though being careful not to be too obvious about it, was watching Berman and Colvert with great interest.

"We been after this son of a bitch for going on six years now, Glenn," said Moss Berman, his voice still low, "and I got a damn good record as a lawman, and all I get on Bill Pigeon from you is a bunch of hoodoo stories. Now, that there body over there looks a hell of a lot like Bill Pigeon to me."

Just then one of the crowd spoke out.

"Hey, how the hell does he know who this is?"

Glenn Colvert turned to face the man.

"Fellows," he said, "this here's United States Marshal Moss Berman. You've all heard of him. I reckon he ought to know Bill Pigeon when he sees him—even in that shape."

Berman turned to walk back to his horse, and Colvert followed him. As they mounted up, they could hear the conversation continuing behind them.

"That there's Moss Berman?"

"Bill Pigeon, huh?"

"Well, I be goddamned."

As Moss Berman and Glenn Colvert rode away from the scene, they heard a loud screech from the top of a tall cottonwood that was standing nearby. They paid it no mind, but back in the crowd, Turtle Brashears turned his head toward the tree, and his keen eyes found, sitting on one of the topmost branches, a great horned owl, and he smiled.

The Night
George Wolfe Died

George Wolfe was on his way home from a meeting of the National Legislature of the Cherokee Nation, to which he had been elected to represent his home district of Goingsnake. The citizens of Goingsnake District, at least a majority of them, had thought that George, a full-blood Cherokee who was fluent in both Cherokee and English and owned his own business, a mildly prosperous general store, would represent all Cherokees well in this time of great tribulation. The United States government was exercising ever-increasing pressure on the small nation, and whites were moving into the Nation in great numbers.

The meeting itself, George's first, had gone well enough, but George was walking away from it with mixed feelings. True, he had been a storekeeper for some time, he had a good education, and he was learning more and more to live like a white man. This night represented his greatest triumph to date, yet George felt an emptiness. He remembered his father, who had lived all his life in the old way, had never taken a white man's name, never worn a white man's suit, and never let his whiskers grow. He had always remained Tsalagi, one of the Real People, and he had had a good life. George knew that, and he wondered if he were not betraying his traditions and his father by doing so well in a life modeled on that of the yoneg—the white man.

He was moving toward his wagon, lost in these thoughts, when he ran into someone.

"Excuse me, Sir. I'm very sorry," he said.

"Yeh? Well, whyn't ya watch where the hell y're going?"

Yoneg, thought George, *drunken* gule.

"I shall in the future, Sir. Please forgive me," he said.

"Goddamn Indin all dressed up. Shit."

"Excuse me," said George.

"Wait just a goddamn minute here, Indin," said the drunk.

"It's late, Sir. I'm on my way home."

"I wanna talk to you, son of a bitch."

As George tried to walk around him, the drunk grabbed him by the shoulders and shoved him hard against the wall of the building in front of them. George took hold of the drunk's wrists in order to wrench them loose, but the drunk pulled one of them away and made it into a fist, which he shoved into George's stomach. Both George's hands went to his middle, and he doubled over. The drunk, having hit him once, and having enjoyed it, decided to hit some more. His fists went everywhere. George kept his back to the wall, stayed doubled up, and did his best to protect himself with his hands and arms until he could catch his breath. Then, clenching both fists together at about the level of his knees, George took careful aim and delivered a terrible double-barreled uppercut to the big man's chin. The white man straightened up slowly and gracefully. His eyes glazed. He began to go over backward in a beautiful, acrobatic backbend. His shoulders hit the dirt and his feet flew up off the ground. Then his whole, huge body settled into the dust.

George wiped some blood off his face with the back of his hand. He was unsteady on his feet, so he leaned back again against the side of the building and took a couple of deep breaths. He was about to turn and go on his way when he heard footsteps, followed by the metallic click of the hammer being pulled back on a double-action revolver.

"All right. Let's don't have no more trouble here. Just come along with me nice and quiet-like."

George did, and he spent the night in jail. He was not allowed to explain things. No explanation was called for. He was Indian and the other man was white. The lawman, too, was white.

When the deputy marshal opened the cell door the next day and said, "All right, Indian, get on out of here, and watch your step from here on," George said, "Ge ga, yo-neg," and it was not George Wolfe who walked out of the jail, for that name stayed behind him in the cell, and he never spoke another word of English.

Wickliffe

Walking the long, dirt road that wound through the hills outside of Gideon, Bennie was beginning to have second thoughts. It was a hot, still night, the locusts were roaring, and the road was rocky. It was so dark that Bennie could not see the face of his pocket watch to tell what time it was, but he guessed that it was two or two-thirty in the morning. At the rate they were going, it would be daylight before they made it home, especially with Lizzie hanging on to him the way she was. And Bennie didn't like to think about facing her parents at daybreak after having kept her out all night.

"We're going to be walking all night," he said.

"I don't mind. I like walking with you," said Lizzie, and she hugged his arm closer to her body.

"We should have left when them other guys left with the team. We'd of had a ride then."

"You wasn't in such a hurry then," said Lizzie.

Bennie didn't answer. *She's right*, he thought. *I wasn't in such a hurry then, at least not to get home.*

Bennie had turned down the wagon ride they were offered earlier, pretending that he wanted to stay longer at the dance. Then when the wagon left, he had talked Lizzie into leaving the dance with him. They had gone into the woods and made love in the grass beside Fourteen-Mile Creek, and Bennie had said, "I love you," and given Lizzie a ring. He had not given her the ring just so she would make love to him. He had not done that. But walking down the hot, dusty road, his skin feeling sticky from the heat and the lovemaking and itchy from having rolled naked on the ground, and feeling the ticks on his body but lacking the light to pick them off, and knowing that he had not yet walked half-way home but worrying about Lizzie's parents, he was having second thoughts.

"Bennie?" Lizzie said, breaking the silence.

"Hmm?"

"What are you thinking about?"

"Oh, nothing. I'm just tired, I guess."

"Bennie?"

"What?"

"We can stop right up there at the top of the hill. We don't have to walk all night. We can spend the night at my friend Lou Ann's house."

Lou Ann lived in a small log house on top of the hill. There was no light in the house when Lizzie and Bennie reached it, but Lizzie went right up to the door and pounded on it and called out something in Cherokee. Bennie, though he was half Cherokee, had been raised with the English language, so he did not understand what was said. Then he heard a woman's voice from inside the house, also speaking Cherokee.

"She'll be here in a minute," said Lizzie.

Bennie felt uneasy, and he thought it was probably because of the language. Lizzie's parents did not speak English either. *Yes,* he thought, *it must be the language that's bothering me.* Then a light appeared inside the house and soon the door opened. The old woman who opened the door talked to Lizzie in Cherokee. She smiled and nodded and spoke to Bennie, and he forced a smile and nodded back to her. He felt like an intruder, not in the old woman's home, but in the world of both women. Their skin was dark, his light. Their hair was black, his light brown. Their eyes were dark brown, nearly black, his were grey. Their language was Cherokee, his English.

While Bennie was thus involved with his own thoughts, the two women continued to talk in Cherokee. Lou Ann boiled some coffee and produced some cold biscuits. Soon the three of them sat down at the table. Bennie took a biscuit and raised it to his mouth, but Lizzie put her hand on his and stopped him. Lou Ann broke off a piece of her biscuit, took it along with her coffee cup, went to the door, and stepped outside. Bennie watched as she dropped the bit of biscuit and then poured some of the coffee out onto the ground. He heard her say a few words in Cherokee. Then she came back inside and sat down, and they ate.

It was then that it all became clear to Bennie. It was not the skin color and it was not the language that had been causing his second thoughts. It was a whole system of beliefs. Bennie had been raised a Christian, and even that religion was to his mind nonsense. This other, which so many of the full-blood Cherokees held to, seemed to him nothing but a vague collection of superstitions. He had pledged his love to this woman earlier the same night, but he could see now that they could never have a life together. He knew now that he must undo what he had done so hastily before, but he didn't want to bring it up in front of Lou Ann, even though she wouldn't understand what was being said. So he waited. Soon Lou Ann had made two pallets on the floor, and he noticed that the heads of the pallets, like that of Lou Ann's own bed, were placed toward the east. Lou Ann put out the light, and they all went to bed. Bennie decided that he would try to put all his problems out of his mind and get some sleep. Just then Lizzie inched her pallet over closer to his and snuggled up beside him.

It seemed to Bennie that he had just dropped off to sleep when he heard an awful commotion outside the house. It was a mixture of the sounds of human voices, horses' hooves, and the barks and yelps of dogs. Bennie sat up, alert. Lizzie came slowly up, rubbing her eyes. Lou

Ann was trying to get her lamp lit. Suddenly there was a banging on the door and a loud rough voice from outside.

"Hello in there. Anybody home?"

Lou Ann got the lamp lit.

"Open up in there. This is the law."

Lou Ann gave Lizzie and Bennie a questioning look.

"Laws?" she said.

Lizzie said something to her in Cherokee.

"We better see who it is," said Bennie.

Lou Ann went to the door and eased it open and a big white man pushed his way through and right past her, striding to the center of the room.

"I'm Deputy U.S. Marshal Gilstrap," he said. "Who's the owner of this here house?"

Gilstrap was a huge man. He was wearing a long slicker, tall boots with his trouser legs tucked inside, and a wide-brimmed hat. He had two revolvers strapped to his hips and was holding a Winchester rifle in his right hand. Above a great handlebar moustache a pair of beady blue eyes shifted nervously about the room. Bennie gestured toward Lou Ann.

"This is her house," he said.

"Yeah?" said Gilstrap. "And who're you?"

"Just friends stopped by for the night."

Gilstrap turned to Lou Ann.

"Well, you're going to have more company tonight than you bargained for. I've got a tired posse outside and a long trail ahead of us tomorrow. We'll sleep here."

Lou Ann looked at Lizzie, and Lizzie said something to her in Cherokee. Lou Ann turned to Gilstrap.

"No room," she said.

So, thought Bennie, *she can talk some English.*

"We'll stay," said Gilstrap as he strode back to the door and opened it. "Boys, get them animals taken care of and come on in. We'll bed down here."

Lou Ann wrapped herself up tight in the quilt from her bed and sat upright on the bed, her back against the wall, scowling as the strange white men filled her little house.

Bennie and Lizzie moved their pallets over against the wall in the corner next to Lou Ann's bed. Bennie did not try to count the men, but soon the floor was filled with them laid out on their bedrolls. Gilstrap took the lamp with him to the spot he had reserved for himself, not far from where Bennie and Lizzie lay.

"We'll be up and at it bright and early, boys," he said as he turned out the light.

There was some rustling around in the dark, and Bennie supposed that Gilstrap was undressing for bed, and soon the room was filled with the heavy body odor of the men, who had been riding hard, and with the sounds of their snores and wheezes. Bennie gave up on the idea of getting any sleep that night. He lay awake with his eyes wide open, staring into the darkness. He was annoyed at the fix he had gotten himself into with Lizzie. He wished that he had not given her the ring. He wanted it back. He was angry at the huge posse of lawmen filling the air in the small house with their snores and their stifling odors. And the longer he lay awake, the angrier he got. Then Lizzie spoke.

"Bennie?"

"What?"

"Bennie, are you going to come in the house with me while I tell my folks?"

"Tell your folks?"

"About us, silly."

"No. No, I can't."

"Why not?"

"Lizzie, I been thinking about this. I'm sorry I got it started. It ain't going to work."

"Why not?"

"You and me, we're too different. I can't even talk to your folks and your friends. I feel like I don't belong here."

"You don't need to feel like that. They don't feel that way about you."

Bennie was quiet for a bit.

"It just ain't going to work," he said. "It ain't just that I can't talk Cherokee. It's all that other stuff you do—all that stuff you believe in."

"You think I'm stupid, don't you?"

"No, I don't think you're stupid, but I do think you've been raised with a lot of damn silly superstitions, and I can't live with that."

Lizzie moved away from Bennie as far as she could, which wasn't far. She pressed herself against the wall.

"Lizzie?"

She didn't answer.

"Give me back the ring."

"No."

"Come on. Give it to me."

"You go to hell," she said, and she stood up and started toward the door. She started toward the door, but it was a slow start. It was dark. She had to step over Bennie, but she stepped on him instead. Bennie grabbed her by the ankle.

"Let me go," she said.

"Where do you think you're going?"

"Let go."

"Give me the ring back."

"No."

Lizzie tried to pull her leg free while Bennie struggled to hang on to her and at the same time stand up so that he could get a better hold on her. As he got halfway to his feet, he reached up with one hand to grab her by the arm, then he released her ankle, but she spun suddenly and tore loose from him, falling backward. She tripped over someone and landed hard on someone else. She screamed. There was a loud yell from beneath her. Suddenly the little room was filled with commotion.

"What the hell's going on?"

"Goddamn it."

"Get off me."

Finally someone lit the lamp, and the room looked for an instant to Bennie like a mass of squirming bodies. Suddenly the large imposing figure of Gilstrap sprang upright from the writhing mass of bodies. He seemed to loom ten feet tall. His hair and moustache were wild. He had nothing on save his long johns and his gun belt, and he had a gun in each hand.

"You're under arrest," he roared. "Every goddamned one of you. I'm taking you all in first thing in the morning. But right now, by God, go back to sleep and keep quiet."

Bennie did not get his ring back that night, and there was no more disturbance. When everyone awoke in the morning, Gilstrap seemed to have forgotten about having arrested them. No one mentioned it. Instead Gilstrap demanded that Lou Ann provide breakfast for his entire mob. She tried to refuse, but Gilstrap was not a man to be refused. Lizzie helped her prepare it. When the posse had eaten, Gilstrap ordered them all outside to prepare for their trek. He alone of the posse remained in the house. He walked over to Lou Ann and looked her hard in the face.

"Now, listen to me, woman," he said. "I believe you understand every word I say, but in case you don't, ask this one here."

He gestured toward Lizzie.

"I'm on the trail of Charlie Wickliffe and his boys. He's wanted by the U.S. government. He's a killer. I know you damned Indians know where he is, and you try to protect him. This is his neck of the woods, and it's yours. So you know where he's at. And you're going to tell me."

Bennie recognized the name. Everyone knew of Charlie Wickliffe. He was wanted by the United States as an outlaw. He had killed some deputies. Nobody seemed to know exactly why he had killed the first deputy, but after that he had killed the ones who came after him. The lawmen couldn't catch up to him in the hills, and it was generally figured that other Cherokees helped him evade the law, warned him of their movements, hid him out, and lied to his pursuers. The Cherokees didn't consider him an outlaw at all. They considered him a patriot. He was a member of the Nighthawk Keetoowahs and was fighting to keep the Cherokee Nation for the Cherokees, fighting against the allotment of Cherokee lands to individuals, fighting against the movement for statehood. Mainly, it seemed, the Cherokees thought that Charlie Wickliffe was fighting to allow them all to remain Cherokee.

Lou Ann looked at Lizzie, then she looked back at Gilstrap.

"Don't know," she said.

Gilstrap bit his lip. He looked at Lizzie.

"Does she know what I said?" he asked.

Lizzie spoke to Lou Ann in Cherokee, and Lou Ann answered her.

"She knows," said Lizzie, "but she don't know where Charlie is. None of us do. He hides out in the hills."

Gilstrap stared at Lizzie. His face turned red with anger. Suddenly he turned back to Lou Ann, swinging his long left arm, and he slapped her across the face with the back of his hand. Immediately his right hand was filled with a pistol, and he shoved it menacingly in Lou Ann's face. Blood trickled out of a corner of her mouth. If Gilstrap looked for fear in the old woman's face, he was disappointed. Her eyes narrowed and her jaw set and she stared him straight in the eyes.

"I don't know where Charlie's at," she said, "but I hope you do find him, 'cause when you do, he gonna shoot you right between the eyes."

Gilstrap cursed and took his posse away. Lou Ann cleaned her house from top to bottom. Bennie got his ring back from Lizzie, and everybody went back to their day-to-day lives. A few days went by. Bennie had not seen Lizzie since the wild, eventful night at Lou Ann's house. He found himself passing some idle hours in town one afternoon, so he picked up a newspaper and went inside a cafe for a cup of coffee. Glancing through the paper, he noticed a headline, "DEPUTY KILLED." He spread the paper out on the table to read.

The body of Deputy U.S. Marshal I. F. Gilstrap was found yesterday in the hills east of Salina. Two bloodhounds, killed by gunshots, had been placed on top of his body. Gilstrap was known to have been on the trail of Charlie Wickliffe, a Cherokee wanted for the murders of other deputies, and it is assumed that Wickliffe is responsible for the murder. Gilstrap was killed by one gunshot wound right between his eyes.

Bennie leaned back in his chair.

"Right between the eyes," he said out loud. His hands went inside the pocket of his jacket and found the ring he had been carrying there. He closed his fingers on the ring.

"I wonder," he said. "I wonder."

The Hanging of Mose Miller

*Mose Miller was a full-blood Cherokee who was hanged for mur-
der in 1894. Most of the rest of the story that follows is fanciful. I
suspect, however, that it is closer to the truth than some of the
outrageous, undocumented, "historical" versions that have appeared in the pulp pages of Wild West magazines.*

March, 1894, Outside of Braggs, Cherokee Nation

Mose Miller sat down against the trunk of a large tree.
He pushed his hat back on his head, cranked a shell into
the chamber of his Winchester, and rested it against his
knees. Across the clearing from the clump of trees in
which he was concealed was a small frame house. It was
early morning. The sun was not yet up and there was no
light in the house.

The house he was watching was the home of a deputy
U.S. marshal whom Mose referred to only as "the Half-
breed." When Mose did not like a man, he refused to say
his name. The Half-breed was half Cherokee Indian and
half white, and though he officially engaged only in the
business of apprehending criminals or alleged criminals,
because of his Cherokee blood he was being used by the
federal government to further the dirty work of the Dawes
Commission. The Dawes Commission was busily engaged
in the overwhelming task of drawing up a new tribal roll

for the Cherokee Nation, but the roll itself was not the goal of the commission. It was only a means toward the final goal, which was the utter dissolution of the Cherokee Nation and the formation of the state of Oklahoma. The roll was to be used for the individual allotment of Cherokee tribal land—a practice repugnant to traditional Cherokees—and would become known eventually as "the Final Cherokee Roll."

The traditional Cherokees were strongly opposed to the work of the Dawes Commission, and under the leadership of the Nighthawk Keetoowah Society, they were working diligently against it. They urged Cherokees not to enroll, and one of the new tasks of the U.S. marshals and their deputies in the Cherokee Nation became to trump up criminal charges against the "troublemakers"—that is to say, against the most vocal of the Nighthawks. Suddenly there emerged several full-blood Cherokee "outlaws," each said by the government to have committed "numerous outrageous crimes," though the crimes were seldom specified. Their ranks included Charley Wickliffe, his brothers, Ned Christie, and Mose Miller—all Nighthawk Keetoowahs.

At about the crack of dawn the Half-breed opened the front door of his house and stepped out onto the porch. Mose took careful aim and rapidly fired three shots. The Half-breed's body fell back into the house. Mose disappeared into the woods.

Mose Miller went with some friends to a dance near Braggs. He hadn't been there long before Andy Pettit approached him with a jug of whiskey.

"Have a drink," offered Andy.

"Thanks, but I better not," said Mose, thinking to himself, *white man's whiskey,* and recalling that he was using Indian medicine to protect himself from the lawmen and that the use of any form of alcohol was strictly forbidden to one using medicine.

"Hinton's finest," said Andy, "from over by Tahlequah. Come on. It'll do you good."

Mose thought it over. It was against his better judgment. It was against his religious beliefs. It was risky. He was tired and tense.

"Ah, what the hell," he said, and he drank.

When Mose woke up from his drunken stupor, he found himself lying on a cot in a dank cell in the Muskogee jail.

Young Henry Starr walked into the jail in Muskogee carrying a paper bag. He stopped in front of the desk. The guard—one Mose had named High Pockets—looked up from his chair.

"I'd like to visit Mose Miller," said Young Henry.

"What's your name?"

"Henry Starr."

"Henry Starr?"

"Oh, I ain't *the* Henry Starr," said Young Henry. "I'm his nephew."

"What's that?" said High Pockets, gesturing toward the bag.

Young Henry held the bag out for High Pockets to inspect.

"Just some smoking tobacco," he said.

When High Pockets was satisfied that Young Henry was not smuggling weapons into jail for Mose, he took him back to the cell and locked him inside.

"Holler when you're done," he said, and he went back to the office to his desk.

"'Siyo, chuj," said Mose, holding out his hand for the younger man to shake.

"'Siyo, eduji," said Young Henry. "Ahaniduh jola."

Mose took the paper bag.

"Redbird made it," said Young Henry.

"Wado," said Mose, and he placed the paper bag on the cot and invited Starr to sit down and have a long talk with him.

Mose was lying on his back on the damp cot in his cell. His hands were folded behind his head. His legs were crossed. He was relaxed—composed. He heard a door open and close, and footsteps came down the hall. Rat Face and High Pockets approached the door of his cell. Rat Face was carrying a shotgun. He backed up against the wall in the hallway and held the shotgun aimed in Mose's general direction.

"Today's your day, you bastard," he said.

"Knock it off," said High Pockets. He was carrying a length of rope and a ring of keys. As he unlocked the cell and stepped inside he noticed the strong, heavy smell of tobacco smoke hanging in the air. It made him slightly nauseated. Mose glanced at Rat Face.

"Tomorrow might be your day," he said, "and I might be around to watch."

"Shit. You're dead, Indian."

"Carl, knock it off," said High Pockets. "Stand up, Miller. It's time to go."

Mose stood up. He looked High Pockets straight in the eyes and High Pockets felt a sudden chill.

"Turn around," he said.

Mose turned his back while High Pockets bound his hands behind him.

"All right, let's go."

Mose walked out the cell door, and the two guards fell in, one on each side of him. They walked to the far end of the hallway that ran between the cells, the end opposite the office, and High Pockets unlocked the door, which led to the yard out back. As he opened the door, the noise of the crowd could be heard.

"Step outside," he said.

Mose stepped outside. He stopped and surveyed the crowd. He looked at the gibbet, then looked off into the distance and squinted his eyes slightly, as if trying to see something there. High Pockets noticed and wondered what he was looking at—or for. He also noticed as a very slight smile appeared on Mose's lips. He looked again in the direction Mose was looking, but he saw nothing—nothing but clear sky above the trees. Then he was suddenly almost overcome by the return of the heavy smell of tobacco smoke. It was as if Mose's body and clothes were permeated with the smoke, and out in the fresh air it was all the more noticeable. High Pockets shuddered. He felt slightly dizzy.

"Let's go," he said.

"Move it, Indian," said Rat Face.

Mose walked steadily and deliberately toward the steps that led up to the platform. When he reached the steps, he felt High Pockets take hold of his arms. Mose stopped.

"I don't need no help, High Pockets."

High Pockets let go and Mose walked up the steps. The crowd became silent as the marshal read the death warrant, and Mose studied faces in the crowd while he waited. He had a look of scorn on his face. The marshal finished reading, folded the paper, and put it in his pocket.

"Mose Miller," he said, "do you have any last words before this execution is carried out?"

"All these people came here to see a show," said Mose. "Let's get on with it."

He looked off into the distance again, and as he felt the noose lowered over his head and the knot tightened against the back of his neck just below his right ear, he could see the shape in the sky growing larger. The marshal drew a black hood out of his pocket.

"No hood," said Mose. "I don't want to miss the show."

The hawk was flying just overhead.

"Be seeing you, Rat Face," said Mose.

"Pull, damn it," said Rat Face.

There was a loud fluttering as the hawk lowered itself and perched on the gibbet just over Mose's head, and an audible gasp came from the crowd. High Pockets noticed that in the split second before the executioner pulled the handle to release the trap a glazed look appeared in Mose's eyes, and he saw Mose's knees buckle slightly just before the trap fell and the body plunged. The hawk screeched and flew away.

"Jesus Christ," said High Pockets.

Rat Face was staring at the body. Beads of sweat had appeared on his forehead.

"He didn't kick or jerk or nothing," he said. "Just dropped like a sack of flour."

"He was dead before he fell," said High Pockets. Then he looked off in the direction the hawk had flown. "At least, I think he was."

Rat Face came out of the outhouse. He was still fastening his breeches as he walked along the path. Suddenly he heard a laugh come seemingly out of nowhere. At least he thought it was a laugh, but as he turned his head quickly to look around, he saw no one. Instead he heard a loud flutter of wings, and he looked up just in time to see a large hawk diving for his face. He screamed and fell down as the hawk screeched and passed over him. It made a graceful turn and circled around to land on the chimney of the house at the end of the path Rat Face was walking. Rat Face raised himself up onto his elbows, and stared down the path at the hawk. As Rat Face stared, the hawk screeched once more. The sound was piercing even though the hawk was some distance away. The sound of the screech was still ringing in Rat Face's ears, and he could still feel the effects of the force of it in his chest when a new sound imposed itself on his bewilderment—a rattle just off to his right. He looked. A large rattlesnake lay coiled. Its mouth was open. It flicked its tongue. Its fangs were long and dripping with venom. When it struck, it struck hard and fast, and its fangs went deep into the flesh of Rat Face's neck just below his ear. He screamed again and grabbed his neck, rolling over onto his right side. He began to sob, and the last sound he heard as he felt the life seeping out of his body was the sound of a long laugh in the air above him.

The Witch of Goingsnake

Bill Brown was what most of the town Cherokees of the western Cherokee Nation in the 1890s called a "conservative" Cherokee. There were those of the people back in the hills, of course, who thought differently. They were the real conservatives—the ones who did their best, in spite of the whites and their own "progressive" people, to live in the old ways according to the ancient teachings of Keetoowah. These Cherokee would have called Bill Brown a progressive, and they would not have meant it as a compliment. The town Cherokees who called Bill Brown a conservative didn't mean it either as a compliment or as an insult. It was just the truth as they saw it.

Bill Brown, the conservative Cherokee, was a tall, powerful man who worked a little farm in the Goingsnake District of the Cherokee Nation in what is now northeast Oklahoma. The farm he worked was not far from a small town called Baptist and not far from Goingsnake Courthouse. Bill Brown did not own his farm, for all Cherokee people, officially all Cherokee citizens, held the land in common. The progressive Cherokees and the traditional, or conservative, Cherokees agreed at least on that one point. The conservatives did not, however, think of themselves in terms of "citizenship," and that was another reason Bill Brown's tag of "conservative" was accurate only from a certain point of view. Bill Brown worked his farm, voted in Cherokee National elections (another activity the real conservatives—the traditionalists—kept away from), read the newspapers (*The Cherokee Phoenix*, written in the Sequoyah syllabary), sent his son to Tahlequah to attend the Cherokee Male Seminary, and dressed himself in his best suit and tie to attend church every Sunday—the Baptist Church, at Baptist, of course—where services were held in the Cherokee language.

But Bill Brown *was* a conservative. What made him a conservative was that, even with all the trappings of "civilization" he had acquired, he for some reason still held on to certain of the old beliefs—the superstitions, some would say. He had been known on more than one occasion to pay for the services of *didahnuwisgi*—conjurers, shamans, or witch doctors, to some. He also clung steadfastly to the Cherokee language, refusing to learn English—or at least refusing for the most part to use it. And he retained his belief in witches. Yes, witches. *Tsgili.* Bill Brown had a great fear of *tsgili*. His progressive friends ridiculed him regularly concerning this fear, but to no avail. He would not be persuaded that they did not exist—that they were mere superstition. Not his best friends, not the principal chief of the Cherokee Nation, not, in fact, the Baptist Church itself could convince Bill Brown that his belief was false and childish. Bill Brown was a conservative Cherokee.

Down the road a short distance from the house where Bill Brown and his family lived, there lived an old woman called Tewa, the Flying Squirrel. Tewa was known to be a conjuring woman. People often took their troubles to her and paid her to make a charm for them or to cure their ills. Some of the more progressive Cherokees simply chuckled at Tewa and her customers, although a few of them went to her on the sly with their own problems. Bill Brown was convinced that Tewa was a *tsgili*—a witch. And he lived in almost constant fear of her proximity to his own home.

One spring morning as Bill was on his way out the front door to go into his field to work, he happened to look up. Just as he was about to step off the front porch, he saw

Tewa, walking down the road that wound by his farm and on down into the woods. She said nothing. She did not stop. She was simply walking down the road on the way back to her own house from somewhere. But as she passed by his house, and just as he looked up and noticed her, Tewa shot a quick glance at him that sent a shudder through his entire, huge frame. She went on. He caught his breath and went on off the porch and around to the back. About an hour later Bill was walking behind his big, brown mule guiding the plow when the blade struck a large rock, and as Bill lunged forward, his weight on the handle of the plow caused the right handle to snap, and he was sent sprawling into the dirt on his face.

"Goddamn," said Bill Brown. (On certain occasions, when there were simply no Cherokee words to fit the need, Bill used a few English words.)

He was getting back to his feet and dusting himself off when he heard a commotion in the patch of woods behind him. He got up and loped over to the edge of the woods. There was a loud rustling of leaves almost at his feet, and his heart skipped a beat. He looked around quickly and saw a squirrel scamper up the trunk of the tall oak nearest him. It reached a branch well above his head, but not so high that he was unable to see it, and then it stopped. Its tail twitched quickly six or seven times; then, in almost imperceptible movements, it turned around on the branch and looked down into his eyes. Beads of sweat appeared on Bill Brown's brow as he stood transfixed, returning the squirrel's gaze.

"Tewa," he said in a barely audible voice.

Then, suddenly—perhaps it ran, its movements were so very quick—the squirrel seemed to just disappear. Bill stood still for a few seconds more, then he backed up three, four steps, turned, and ran back into the field to his plow and mule. He unhitched the mule and, leaving the broken plow there in the field, drove the mule hurriedly back to its corral behind the house. He went inside and dropped the bar across the door, the sweat running down his face, which was as pale as it could possibly get. His wife, Sarah, looked up from the table where she was busy cleaning wild onions. She could see that he was upset.

"Wil," said Sarah, "what's wrong with you? What's happened?"

"Tewa," Bill said. "Tewa passed by here this morning."

"So?"

"She gave me a look as she passed, and it made me shiver, but I went on to work anyway."

"Is that all?" said Sarah. "You must stop worrying so over Tewa. She is just a poor old woman."

"No," said Bill, "that was not all. In the field my plow broke and I was thrown. And there was this squirrel watching me. It was the *tsgili*."

"Sit down, Wil," said Sarah. "Let me get you some coffee."

"Where is An?"

"She is at school, of course. Where should she be on a school day?"

Sarah brought Bill his coffee. He took a quick sip and, finding it too hot, slopped some into his saucer and blew on it.

"Something bad will happen," he said, and he slurped the coffee from the saucer.

Then he got up from the chair and put his cup and saucer back down on the table. He went to the chest of drawers across the room and took a pistol from the top drawer, then a box of shells, and began to load the pistol.

"Gado haduhne? What are you doing?" asked Sarah.

"I'm going to the school to get An."

"Why? Why will you do that?"

"Something bad will happen. I must have her here at home where I can watch over both of you."

Bill jammed the pistol into the waistband of his trousers and hurried out the door. In less than an hour he was home again with An, his nine-year-old daughter. He pounded on the door and shouted to his wife to let them in, for he had ordered her to replace the bar after him when he left. Sarah let them in, and Bill again barred the door. Only then did he sit down and have a cup of hot coffee. It settled his nerves a bit; however, he kept the loaded pistol in his lap. Sarah and An finished cleaning the onions.

"I'm going out to the field for my plow," said Bill, again tucking the pistol into his pants. "I must mend it this afternoon so I can work tomorrow. Already I have lost one day. The corn can't wait forever to be planted—Tewa or no. You two stay inside. I won't go far, and I won't stay long."

Halfway out to the field, Bill stopped and rubbed his eyes. *No*, he thought, *it can't be*. But the plow was not to be seen. He ran to the spot where he had abandoned it earlier, and there he found the piece of handle which had broken off, but nothing else. He picked up that piece and was looking at it helplessly when he heard the rustling leaves in the oak tree. He looked, and there, staring at him from the same branch, was the squirrel.

"Goddamn you," he shouted in English, and he jerked the pistol from his trousers and fired five shots. The first one struck the squirrel in the center of the face and tore most of its head off. The second hit its soft belly and flipped it backward through the air. The other three went wild.

"That's all of that," Bill said nervously to himself, and, pistol in one hand, broken plow handle in the other, he walked back to his house.

"That's all of that," he said again.

Nevertheless, Bill Brown did not sleep well that night.

The following morning, Bill got up early. Although he had shot the squirrel, he was no longer sure that it had been the right squirrel—that it had been Tewa. Probably, he thought, had it really been the *tsgili*, his bullets would not have hurt it. He bade Sarah to keep An home from school one more day and cautioned her to stay inside the house and keep the door barred during his absence. He hitched the mule to his wagon and drove into Baptist, where he had the storekeeper order him a new plow. On his way back home, he stopped by the farm of his friend George Fox. Bill and George often rode together on posses for the sheriff of Goingsnake District when he needed their help. George was plowing.

"Well, Farmer Brown," said George, "have you gotten so rich that you don't need to work anymore now?"

"My plow was broken yesterday, and then it disappeared," said Bill. "I had to go to town and order a new one, but I'm afraid that it will be too late this year when the new plow comes."

"When I am done with my plowing," said George, "you can take this one to use."

"Wado," said Bill. "Thank you."

"But what do you mean your plow disappeared? Is it stolen?"

"I wish it had been stolen," said Bill. "I think it was taken by the *tsgili*."

Then he told George the events that had made him suspicious of Tewa. He did not, however, tell of killing the squirrel.

"My friend," said George when Bill had finished his tale, "I believe that you are too superstitious. Perhaps Tewa is a *tsgili*. I do not know, but I rather doubt it. I know that many believe in her conjuring, but I think that she's just a shrewd old woman. I think that you've been frightened by a series of coincidences—rather strange ones, for sure—but coincidences nonetheless, and because of your superstition you have imagined that Tewa is after you. Your plow has been stolen, I think."

Bill shook his head slowly.

"I hope that you're right," he said, "but I fear not."

"When I've finished with my plowing, I'll bring this plow to your house. Don't worry about Tewa. It's all in your head. I'm sure of it."

Three nights later Bill Brown was awakened from a sound sleep by a terrible commotion in back of his house. There were sounds of scuffling and of snorting and squealing. He hurriedly got out of bed, lit the kerosene lamp, grabbed his pistol, and ran out into the night. The commotion was coming from his corral, and when he rounded the house, he discovered a large wild hog just in the process of finishing off his mule. The mule had put up a valiant fight, but it was no match for the razorback. Its throat had been ripped open, and it hardly had enough strength left to even try to defend itself. Bill fired his pistol into the thick hide of the hog. The hog snapped its head back as if it thought something had bitten it. Bill fired again, running toward the battle and screaming at the hog. When the second bullet struck the hog, and it realized that Bill was there, it abandoned the kill and ran into the darkness. It was too late. The wretched mule was done for. It was in dreadful agony, and Bill could tell that it would be only a matter of time before the poor animal was dead. He took careful aim with his pistol and, with one shot, put the mule to rest.

Two days later George Fox showed up at the Browns' farm with his plow in a wagon.

"Bill," he said, as Bill came out the front door of his house to see who was there. "I've brought you this plow to use."

"Thank you, friend," said Bill, "but it's too late. My mule is killed now. It's too late to plant my corn."

"Ha," said George, "that's too bad about your mule. How did it happen?"

Bill told him about the wild hog.

"I'm sorry about your mule," said George, "and I know it's late for your corn, but it's not yet too late. Here is a plow for you to use. Put out your corn. Perhaps it will be all right yet."

"But I have no mule to pull the plow."

"I will leave my horse here for you to use until you get your plowing done. I can manage without him for a few days."

"You're a good friend," said Bill, "but I am not going to plow. It's too late. Besides, if you leave your horse here, something may happen to it. Then you would have no horse because of my troubles."

"Nonsense," said George. "You're still thinking that old Tewa is doing this to you, I see. You've had some bad luck is all. Listen. I'll stay and help you plow your field. That way it will be done more quickly, and your corn will have a better chance."

Finally Bill was persuaded, and he and George both went immediately to the field and set to work. They plowed the rest of that day, and George took his plow and horse back home for the night only to return with them early the following morning. The two men worked together all that day, too. They finished the plowing and they planted the seed. George Fox's horse was once more hitched to the wagon standing in the road in front of Bill's house.

"Wado, my friend," said Bill. "Without you I could not have done it."

"Everything will be all right, Bill. You'll see," said George.

Just then the two men heard shuffling footsteps in the dirt road. Someone was approaching from around the bend in the direction of George's house and the town of Baptist, beyond. They waited in silence until they could see the approaching figure amble around the bend. When it came into sight, Bill Brown's heart stopped for an instant. George Fox, in spite of himself, was also stunned briefly, but he quickly regained his composure.

"'Siyo, Tewa," said George, as cheerfully as he could manage.

The old woman nodded and grumbled something under her breath as she came closer. Without saying anything more, or even looking in the direction of the two men, she slowly made her way past the house and on down the road. George went on home, and Bill went inside the house feeling very ill at ease.

It was two days later that little An fell ill. Bill was afraid to leave Sarah and An alone for very long, so he rushed to the home of George Fox, who readily agreed to go for the doctor. When the doctor arrived, he examined the child and administered some medication, but he was not hopeful. He could not be sure, he said, what was wrong with her. He told the worried parents to continue giving her the medicine and said that he would be back to check on her, but he was not hopeful. Two days passed, and little An's condition only grew worse. In desperation, Bill went into the hills and sought out an old Indian doctor. The old man returned to the house with Bill and examined An. He sang over her and gave her some medicine made of herbs. He went outside and drew a ring of tobacco around the house, chanting the whole time. He stood in the road for some time, smoking and blowing smoke down the road, singing the while. When he was finished, he told Bill and Sarah that he had done all he could. His medicine, he was afraid, would not be very effective. Some conjurer had cast a spell on the Browns' house. The conjurer, whoever it might be, was very strong. He had done all he could do. Three days later, An was dead.

Bill and Sarah buried their daughter under a large oak tree behind their house. Bill built a small, wooden frame, like a house, over the grave. He built a roof over the house. The Baptist preacher came and offered a prayer for the child's soul. When all was done and the friends and relatives were gone, Bill took out his pistol again.

"Wil," said Sarah, "what are you doing?"

"I am going to kill that *tsgili*," he said. "I will take no more of this from her. She has done this to us—this and all the rest. Now I am going to kill her for sure."

He took the pistol, checked its load, and left the house. In a few minutes he had walked the distance to Tewa's cabin. It stood under the trees on the edge of the woods, just a few yards back from the winding road. Bill Brown was terribly afraid, but he was also determined. Nervously, he rechecked his pistol. He could see a thin column of smoke rising from the chimney of the cabin there before him. Holding the pistol in his right hand, he drew himself up to his full height and started toward the cabin. When he stepped onto the front porch, his shoes made a clomping sound, and the boards of the porch creaked loudly. He hesitated. Then he heard the voice of the hated old woman from inside the cabin.

"Who is there?" she asked in a creaky voice.

"Tewa," Bill shouted. "Tsgili, ayuh Bill Brown."

He held out the pistol ready for firing, drew himself back, and with all his might, kicked the door. It flew open, swinging all the way back and smashing into the wall. The old woman was at a pot on the fire. She looked up, startled, just in time to see Bill level his pistol at her. She began to scream, and Bill Brown emptied his gun into her body.

The force of the shots threw Tewa away from the fire and back against the far wall of the small room. She lay there in a crumpled heap looking very small—too small, indeed, for the rivers of blood that kept pouring from the horrible, fresh wounds. Bill stood still, staring at the body for a few seconds, his eyes wide. Finally he took two long and hurried steps toward the fireplace and, shifting the empty pistol to his left hand, seized with his right hand the cold end of a flaming hickory faggot. He raced about the room touching flame to anything that would catch fire easily—the drab and dirty curtains on the windows, the worn tablecloth, the bedclothes. Then he hesitated, flames all around him, and stepped to the center of the room. He looked again at the old woman's body. The flames began to crackle. Bill tossed the burning hickory on top of the body and watched until the ragged dress that covered it began to smolder, then he turned and ran from the cabin. He ran across the road and sat down beneath a tree, where he stayed to watch until the cabin had burned to the ground.

The evening of the following day the sheriff of Going-snake showed up at the Brown house and arrested Bill

Brown for Tewa's murder. Bill did not resist. He did not deny the killing. He bade his wife farewell and went peacefully to jail. Bill spent some time in jail awaiting his trial, and during that time, Sarah visited him regularly, but when the day of trial came, she was not there at Goingsnake Courthouse. Bill looked nervously about. He saw his friend, George Fox.

"George, my wife is not here," he said.

"She is ill today, Bill," said George. "I have just now come from your house. I'm sorry, but I'm sure she'll soon be over it. Don't worry. I'll watch over her for you. Right now my wife is with her."

The trial was brief. Bill admitted having done the deed. His only defense was that Tewa was a witch and that she had cast a spell on him and his whole house. She had begun by breaking his plow and making it disappear. She had then sent a wild hog to kill his mule, and finally she had done her worst—she had sent a mysterious illness to take his only daughter from him. The court refused to accept Bill's steadfast belief in witchcraft as grounds for justifiable homicide or to see the killing as self-defense, so Bill was found guilty of murder and sentenced to die by hanging. A date was set. As Bill was being led from the courtroom, George Fox put a hand on his shoulder.

"Don't worry, Bill," he said. "Your friends haven't given up on you yet. Some of us are going to go to Tahlequah to see the chief. Maybe we can get him to pardon you. We'll explain the circumstances to him. I'm sure that when we've shown him that you're no murderer, he'll understand and issue the pardon."

"Don't bother about all that," said Bill. "I know that I'm doomed. But if you want to go to Tahlequah for me, go to the school and get my son. I want to see him once more before I die, and when I'm gone, his mother will need him at home."

"I'll tell him, Bill, but we'll also talk to the chief."

Bill did not see George again until the day that had been set for his hanging. The sheriff came with his two deputies to the cell. They tied Bill's hands behind his back, and they led him out to the hanging tree—a huge oak behind the courthouse. They helped Bill climb into the bed of a wagon that was parked beneath the tree. Dangling above the wagon bed was the noosed hanging rope. Bill stood just beneath the noose. A deputy climbed into the driver's seat with a whip in his hand. The other deputy climbed into the wagon beside Bill and placed a black sack over his head. Then he began to adjust the noose around Bill's neck. Bill did not mind dying. The day before, Martha Fox, George's wife, had come to visit Bill in his cell. She had told him that his Sarah was dead. Bill no longer felt that he had anything to live for. He would have liked to have seen his son one more time, but then he would have been perfectly content to die. He was not at all certain, especially since having heard about Sarah, that the killing of Tewa had put an end to the curse of the *tsgili*. He might as well die. He would have liked to have seen his son once more, but perhaps it was better, he thought, that he had not come. Perhaps, as he was away at school when the curse had been put on the Brown family, it had missed him, and with Bill's death, surely it would come to an end.

The sheriff was reading the death warrant and the deputy had finished adjusting the noose when Bill heard the approach of a fast-running horse.

"Stop it. Stop it. Wait," someone was shouting.

The rider pulled up his horse somewhere very near and began to speak rapidly. Bill recognized the voice of George Fox.

"Wait, Sheriff, I've got a pardon here for Bill."

"What?" said the sheriff. "A pardon?"

"I've just ridden as hard as I could all the way from Tahlequah. I was afraid that I wouldn't get here in time."

"You've got a pardon for Bill Brown?"

"Yes, right here."

"How'd you get that?"

"Well, Sheriff, you know, politics. The chief realizes

that a good many of the people still hold fast to many of our old traditions. Anyhow, it's signed and legal."

"Keep your foot on that brake," said the sheriff. "And you—turn loose the prisoner."

At long last the sack was removed from Bill's head and he was untied. He climbed down from the wagon, and George ran to hug him.

"Bill," said George, "it's over now. Tewa is dead and you are free."

"Wado, George," said Bill, "but where is my boy? I suppose you rode so fast that he could not keep up with you?"

George's face grew long.

"Bill," he said, "I'm so sorry. You've had so much misfortune lately. He's dead, Bill. Killed in Tahlequah by a stray bullet in a gunfight. He was just standing in the wrong spot."

For the next two years of his life, Bill Brown lived alone. He continued to live in his old house with all its painful memories. He continued to plant his field. He seldom left the farm to go to town or to visit friends. In fact, had George Fox not made it a point to drive over to visit him every couple of weeks, Bill would almost have been a hermit. After the first year he did start attending church in Baptist again, but even then he would not pause following the service to chat with his old friends. About eighteen months had passed before he again agreed to ride with the special posses when he was asked. When he went out with the posse the first time, George had worried, but Bill had done his part without any problems. George began to think that perhaps, after all, Bill would be all right.

Bill was forty-two years old the night the posse rode up to his house for the last time. He had just finished his evening meal. The sheriff had come up to the door and knocked. Bill opened the door to the sheriff, and he could see the posse members on horseback waiting in the road.

"We are riding tonight?" he asked.

"Yes," said the sheriff. "Four men robbed the store on

the road to Tahlequah. We've tracked them out this direction. They're armed, and they're pretty mean. We can use your help."

"Of course, I'll go," said Bill, and he got out his pistol.

The posse rode down the road, past the spot where old Tewa's cabin had once stood, and Bill felt his heart begin to pound. He suppressed an urge to stop his mount and inspect the spot. They rode on. It was an hour later when the posse was met on the road by a lone rider.

"Who's that coming?" asked Bill.

"One of us," said George. "We sent him ahead to scout the outlaws."

The sheriff called the posse to a halt, and the rider trotted his mount up to meet them.

"Sheriff," the scout said, "I found them just up ahead. There's an old cabin just on the other side of that hill there. It faces this direction. They're in there. Looks like they're settled in for the night. They've got a fire going, and their horses are unsaddled."

The posse rode up the hillside to just below the crest, and there they dismounted and were divided into four small groups by the sheriff. One group was sent around behind the cabin in case anyone tried to get out that way. One group each was sent to the two other sides of the cabin, and the fourth group stayed in front. In this last group were the sheriff, George Fox, and Bill Brown. The sheriff's group was to give the others time to get into place, and then they would move in on the men in the cabin. When everyone was in position, the group in front crept up close. The sheriff, George, and Bill went quietly up onto the porch of the cabin. The sheriff got on one side of the door, George Fox on the other. Bill stood directly in front of the door but a couple of steps back. All three had their guns in hand.

"You inside," shouted the sheriff in English, for he did not know just who the men were, "you inside, come on out one at a time with your hands up."

Someone inside shouted, "The law," and another, "Goddamn."

Just then Bill kicked in the door. He saw a man go for a rifle, and he dropped him with one shot. A second outlaw quickly raised a shotgun and fired both barrels full into Bill's chest. Bill went flying back out onto the porch. The sheriff rushed into the house and, dodging to one side of the door, shot in the side the man who had fired the shotgun. The outlaw dropped screaming to the floor. A third man was trying to open a back door, but just as he got it unlatched, George Fox sent a bullet smashing into the door over the man's head.

"Hold it," he shouted.

"Don't shoot. Don't shoot," cried the outlaw, darting his hands up over his head. The fourth man was seen to be hugging his knees to his chin behind a table in a corner of the room. As soon as he could see that things were under control, George turned from the room to see about Bill out on the porch. The quiet after the holocaust was almost eerie. Just as George stepped across the threshold to go out the door, something flew by him right in front of his face. He screamed involuntarily and stepped back, his heart pounding. Then he looked in the direction the thing had flown. He saw a squirrel running madly for a nearby oak.

"Tewa," he whispered harshly and in spite of himself.

And Bill Brown breathed his last breath.

Moon Face

Hominy Grits did not like the old woman Moon Face. Moon Face had not ever done anything to bother him. As far as he could tell, she was always minding her own business, and she was friendly enough when she passed by his house. She often passed by his house on her way back and forth on whatever business it was that took her away from home. Hominy Grits could not imagine what business an old woman who lived alone and had no relatives could possibly have that would take her out and away from home so much. Every time she passed by his house, the sight of her out on the road irritated him.

"An old woman like that should stay home," he would tell his wife, Meggie.

"Why do you worry about poor old Moon Face?" Meggie would answer. "She's not doing you any harm by wandering around. She's all alone. She probably doesn't have anything else to do."

"But where is she going all the time?"

"Maybe she's visiting some friends somewhere."

"I don't know anybody around here who is friends with that crazy old woman."

Hominy Grits just didn't like old Moon Face. And Moon Face could tell. She could tell by the look on his face when she passed his house. She would smile and say, "'Siyo," and he would grumble and glare. She knew that he did not like her. She wondered why Hominy Grits did not like her. She wondered what he thought about her and what he might say about her when she had passed by his house. Did he talk about her to his family when they were all inside in the evenings? She became obsessed with these questions. She felt like she simply had to find out what Hominy Grits thought of her and how he talked about her.

One evening, not long after Moon Face had passed by Hominy Grits's house, Meggie called for her husband and children to come in to supper. Hominy Grits leaned his hoe against the side of the house and started to go in.

"Come on," he said to the children, who were playing in the dirt beside the house. "Let's eat."

As he went in the house, he was followed by four children and five cats. No one bothered to count the cats. If they had, they would have noticed that there was an extra cat in the house—a strange cat. It was a slick, black one, and it stayed close to the other cats—huddled up amongst them. The cats all ran to the shallow pan which Meggie had put their dinner in and placed on the floor. Four of the cats were busy eating and shoving each other to get a better spot at the edge of the pan. The black cat simply crouched in the midst of them. Suddenly the youngest of the children, a boy of about two and a half years, made a dash for Meggie, and his path led him straight through the crowd of cats. The four who were on familiar ground knew enough to give him room, but the black cat was caught by surprise. The little one tromped hard on its tail, and the black cat made a screech that caused Meggie to drop a dish and Hominy Grits to almost fall backward in the chair which he had been sitting in rocked back on two legs.

Before anyone had time to say anything about the cat's screech, the cat, furious with pain, clawed the bare leg of the toddler and made his blood run. The poor little boy began to scream in pain and fright. Hominy Grits leapt from his chair and raced for the cat. The black cat was so intent on its revenge that it did not see Hominy Grits coming after it. The cat had latched itself onto the little boy's leg with the claws of all four feet. All the children were screaming. The mother was raving. The cat was hissing and snarling.

Hominy Grits grabbed the black cat by the nape of its neck, and when the cat felt its neck and back skin wadded up in his grip, it writhed and twisted to get its claws into the flesh of this new enemy. Hominy Grits, that cat clawing at his wrist, went to the door and opened it. Then, with all his strength, he flung the black cat at a tree that stood out in front of his house. As soon as he had turned loose of the cat, Hominy Grits turned to a bucket of coals that stood beside the wood stove upon which Meggie had cooked supper. As the cat yowled outside, Hominy Grits grabbed the bucket of glowing coals, ran back to the door, and flung the contents of the bucket at the cat. Many of the coals found their mark, and the yowls and screeches became even more terrible as the black cat disappeared down the road that ran in front of the house.

The next day, just after the family had finished lunch, Hominy Grits announced that they were all going for a walk.

"Where are we going?" asked one of the children.

"Oh," said Hominy Grits, "I think we'll take this left-over food to that old woman who lives down the road."

"What are you up to now?" asked his wife.

"Come on," he said. "Let's go."

When they got to the house of Moon Face, they stopped and stood in the middle of the road. Hominy Grits stared at the house, not feeling as brave as he had before.

"Well," said Meggie, "what now?"

Hominy Grits drew himself up and walked up to the door.

"Moon Face, old woman," he shouted, "are you in there?"

"Who is it?" came a voice from inside.

Hominy Grits's courage returned to him, and he opened the door and stepped inside.

"We brought you some food, old woman," he said.

The old woman was lying in her bed with a quilt covering most of her body, but Hominy Grits could see that her arms, which were lying out on top of the quilt, were bandaged. Her hair was frizzled as if it had been singed, and one bad burn was visible on her face.

"Why, what has happened to you?" asked Hominy Grits.

"Oh, I fell into my fire yesterday," answered the old woman. "It will be all right soon."

Hominy Grits left the food they had brought and went back outside to join his family. After they had walked down the road for a little while, he stopped and turned around facing back toward the old woman's house. Then he looked at his wife.

"So now we know," he said.

The Name

Muskogee, Indian Territory, was a railroad town—not a very old one. Like other railroad towns it brought with it multitudes of people with all kinds of habits—mostly bad. It brought into the Creek Nation gambling, prostitution, more illegal liquor, and much more fighting: fist fights were common, knifings frequent, and shootings not unusual. It was a crowded town full of action. Violence was a way of life in Muskogee, and the reputation it gained attracted more people who liked violent action— aimless people with nothing to lose and, at least many of them thought, everything to gain.

One day a lone outlaw with no name rode into Muskogee on a stolen horse. He was carrying a stolen rifle in the crook of his right arm and had a stolen pistol in his pocket. In the waist band of his trousers was another pistol—a borrowed one. He was a tall, large-boned young man. His skin was yellowish, and he had a shock of curly, dark reddish-brown hair. He wore farmer's brogans, and his clothes were poor, but he rode his handsome mount with ease and dignity. As he rode down the main street of Muskogee, he looked around with mild curiosity, but not with the air of a country boy on his first trip to town. The awe that Muskogee inspired in its visitors was a result of the fear of unexpected violence in a strange town. It was a fear that only those with something to lose felt. The outlaw with no name had nothing to lose. He had a reputation to gain—a vast, romantic reputation—and all the excitement and fun that goes along with gaining it. And he had no fear, for in his eighteen years he had already seen much violence. He had beaten men with his fists and had been beaten. And he had killed two men, or so he thought, and he had committed armed robbery. He looked at Muskogee with mild curiosity. Here his legend would begin. Here in Muskogee. Here would begin the tale of— of the outlaw with no name? No. He must have a name for the storytellers. A name. He thought of the stories he had heard people tell of the outlaws who were most on their minds, stories of Bill Doolin, Bill Dalton, and best of all, Billy Cook. Bill. Bill was an outlaw's name. Bill was better than—well, than no name at all. He would be Bill. It was not enough, but the rest would come.

He rode his horse up to a hitching rail and dismounted. He didn't know where he would go or what he would do. He only knew that here in Muskogee, in the Creek Nation, he was safe from the authorities in the Cherokee Nation, and that he would have time to think—to make some decisions about his new career, to finish his name, and to acquire all the things that must go with it: boots, new clothes, money. The story was begun, but the plot had yet to develop. He tied the horse to the hitching rail, then straightened up to have a look around. There were all kinds of places visible from where he stood—places that would be interesting to look into. There were things to do. There were people everywhere. But he had no money. To go to all of the places he wanted to would require money. It took money to get a drink, money to play cards, money to visit a whore, and money to eat. He was hungry. His stomach was growling at him, and he was afraid someone else would hear it. There was a cafe just across the street from where he stood, but he had no money. He would have to steal some. He leaned back against the hitching rail and watched the people passing by in the street. He carefully selected a well-dressed man driving a natty buggy and heading out of town, then followed him and robbed him of his money.

When Bill rode back into Muskogee later, he had money in his pocket. He rode directly up to the cafe he had noticed before, tied his horse to the rail in front, went inside, and sat down at a table. He ordered an extravagant meal and ate voraciously, washing it down with lots of coffee. When he finished his meal, Bill paid for it and bought five cigars. He put four in his pocket and lit the fifth one, then strolled outside, puffing.

He placed his horse in a livery stable down the street and went into a hotel to get a room for the night.

"Ain't got none," the clerk said. "All full up."

"Any other hotel in town?"

"Yep, but I don't think you'll have any better luck there. Might try around the corner yonder. It ain't exactly a hotel. You'll see a sign out front says, 'beds.'"

Bill thanked the man and left. He walked to the end of the block and turned the corner to a long, low building. Its bare boards had never been painted. Tacked above the door in front was a crudely hand-painted sign. It said only, "BEDS." Bill went inside. A man with three days' growth of beard sat cross-legged on the dirt floor behind a wooden crate that served as his desk. On the crate was a scrap of paper with "PROP." penciled on it.

"You got a bed?" Bill asked.

"I got 'em."

"How much?"

"Twenty-five cents the night and I ain't responsible for no lost, stolen, nor damaged gear. Pay in advance."

Bill drew a twenty-five-cent piece from his pocket and tossed it onto the crate. The "prop." picked it up, took a cigar box out from inside the crate, dropped the twenty-five cents into it, and replaced the box. He gestured with his thumb toward a door behind him.

"Right through there. They's four empty beds right now. Take any one of them."

Bill went through the door and found himself in a long room. It was not lit, and soon, when the sun had gone down, the room would be in total darkness. There were no windows, but some light was creeping in through cracks between boards here and there. On the floor a row of pallets lined each wall. About half of them were occupied. The air was musty. It smelled of tobacco smoke, whiskey, and urine, as well as of unwashed human bodies. Bill could hear heavy breathing and at least one man's snoring. He stood for a moment at the door, adjusting his eyes to the lack of light and accustoming his nostrils and lungs to the air. Then he walked to an empty pallet at the far end of the room. He laid his rifle down between the pallet and the end wall, pulled the pistol out of his waistband, and put it in the opposite jacket pocket from where he carried the other one. He checked what was left of his recently acquired money, also in a jacket pocket, then he rolled the jacket up into a ball and placed it at the head of the pallet to use as a pillow. He sat down on the pallet and pulled off his brogans. Tossing them to the floor by the wall, he stretched out with a loud sigh and closed his eyes to get some sleep. It had been, all in all, a good day, he thought.

Bill was tired and sleepy. He had ridden into Muskogee, then pulled off his first highway robbery. Even the rude pallet felt good to him. He soon ceased to notice the rancid smell of the room, and the snoring and heavy breathing did not bother him for long. Soon he dropped into a state of sleep—or half sleep. He wasn't sure which. He didn't know whether he was dreaming or thinking, but he didn't care. He saw himself astride the horse he had stolen, riding fast across the prairie. His curly hair was blowing behind him in the wind. He wore a bright red shirt and had a flashy bandana tied round his neck: a high-crowned, broad-brimmed, white hat sat with a rakish tilt on his head. As he raced along, the reins held easily in his left hand, a wide smile on his lips, he waved a six-gun in his right hand. Without warning or reason, he began to laugh loudly, and the laughter echoed all around him, and he fired the pistol six, eight, fourteen times. Goddamn, he cut a handsome figure. Then he saw his mother's house ahead of him, and he raced the horse up into the yard and pulled it to a hard, fast stop. "Whoa. Whoa," he shouted, just as the front door of the house flew open to reveal Mama.

"Bill," she shouted, and she ran toward him with arms outstretched, eager for an embrace. Bill whipped the great, white hat off his head, and, dismounting rakishly by bringing his right leg up and over the saddlehorn in front of his body with an easy swing, he hopped lightly out of the saddle and landed softly on the ground. Then he noticed the boots. He was wearing a shining pair of black riding boots—the most beautiful boots he had ever seen. Mama threw her arms around his neck and hugged him with all her strength. When he got himself loose from her, he turned to the fancy saddlebags on his horse and reached inside, drawing out a small, leather bag. "This is for you, Mama," he said, and, loosening the top of the bag, he poured gold coins into her open palms—a great mound of them. They overflowed from her hands and began spilling onto the ground. The tinkling of the falling coins filled the air, and the coins kept falling even when Bill stopped pouring them from the bag. He saw his younger brother running from the woods behind the house carrying his bucket and gig. "Bill. Bill," he shouted. "I heard all about you, Bill. Gosh, I'm proud." Bill said, "Come on, Clarence. I'll show you how to shoot my six-guns." Then he was shooting at the falling coins, which were everywhere in the air, and as his bullets hit them, they bounced and floated, and amidst the pinging of the bullets and tinkling and bouncing and floating of the coins, the girl Maggie Glass floated toward him. Mama and Clarence were no longer there. Only the coins kept floating. Only the tinkling remained in his ears. Bill did not speak, nor did Maggie. She floated right up to him until their lips met in a long kiss, and Bill could see nothing but the float-

109

ing coins in Maggie's eyes and could hear nothing but the tinkling. Then he and Maggie, their lips still pressed together, began to float with the coins. Faster and faster, they drifted through the air. Bill's head was spinning. Then all was dark, his mind was blank, and he slept soundly the rest of the night.

When light once again began to creep through the cracks between the boards, Bill awoke. He looked to his side for his rifle and found it where he had left it. He sat up and started to pull on his brogans, but noticed across the aisle, beside a sleeping white man, a pair of boots. They were not beautiful like the black boots in his dream, but they were boots. Lying under his blanket, the man looked big—about as big as Bill. Bill unrolled his jacket and put it on, picked up the rifle and his cigars, then, carrying his brogans, moved stealthily toward the boots. Their owner seemed sound asleep. Bill lifted one boot and held it beside one of his shoes. *'Bout the same,* he thought. He tried them on. They fit. Close enough, anyway. He quietly put his brogans where the boots had been and left the building. As he walked out, he saw the "prop." asleep at his "desk." Bill made his way back to the same cafe at which he had eaten the night before. Most of Muskogee was still unfamiliar territory.

Inside the cafe he sat down at a table by the front window and ordered four fried eggs, bacon, biscuits, syrup, and coffee. He drank one cup of coffee while waiting for his meal. He checked the money in his pocket. If he were not careful, it would not last long. As his meal was placed before him, a large white man entered the cafe. He looked irritated. He moved to the counter, then looked around the room. His look settled on Bill at the table by the window. The waiter was just about to walk back behind the counter when the man spoke.

"Hey. Hey, you," he said.

Bill was busy sopping a biscuit in syrup. He paid no attention to the man.

"I'm talking to you, you high yella nigger," the man said. "You by the window."

Bill froze, his eyes glaring at the man. The waiter stopped walking and turned back to face the speaker.

"Say," he said, "I don't want no trouble in here."

"That there son of a bitch is wearing my boots."

Bill looked down at the man's feet and recognized his cast-off brogans. He smiled. Two young men on the other side of the room pushed their chairs back from the table and turned to watch.

"You know what he's talking about, mister?" the waiter asked Bill.

"Why, hell, I ain't never seen this man before."

"Them's my damn boots you got on."

"Say," said Bill, "can't a man eat his breakfast in peace in this here place?"

"I want them boots back, boy. Now you pull them off right now, or I'm going to whip your black ass."

Bill jumped up out of his chair and slapped the man three times across the face.

"I'm a Cherokee Indian, you red-neck bastard," he shouted, "and you better apologize to me while you still can."

The big man was surprised, but he recovered quickly, and he kicked the table over at Bill with his left foot while drawing a pistol out of his belt with his right hand.

"Hold on, mister."

The big man stopped, his pistol not quite raised. The voice had come from behind him. One of the two men who had been watching at the other table was pointing a pistol at the big man's back.

"You raise that gun another inch, and I'll kill you."

The man's companion got up and walked over to the big man and took the gun out of his hand.

"Bring it over here, Jimmy," said the one holding the gun at the table.

Bill got up from the floor and stood facing the big man.

"I got his gun, friend," said Jimmy. "You want him to apologize now?"

"He had his chance. It's too late, now."

Bill swung a fist into the big man's stomach, but it didn't do the damage he thought it would. The big man grabbed Bill by the arm and swung him around into the wall, then drove two fists, one after the other, into Bill's ribs. Bill drew his arms in close to his chest to protect his body and raised his fists to his face to cover it. In that manner, he took several more of the man's blows. Then, seeing his chance, he raised a leg and brought a boot heel down as hard as he could on the man's foot. He thought that he felt bones crack. The big man screamed in pain and instinctively reached for his foot. Bill bashed him in the ear sending him staggering backward a few steps. Then he grabbed the nearest chair and swung it hard, dropping the man to the floor like a sack of flour. Bill leaned back against the wall and took a few deep breaths.

"Bravo," said Jimmy, and he ran over to slap Bill on the shoulder.

"Help me throw him out in the street," said Bill.

He took one of the man's arms and Jimmy took the other. They dragged him to the door and heaved him outside. Jimmy tucked the man's pistol into the waistband of his own trousers.

"Come on over and join us," he said. "You gonna have to order a new breakfast, anyhow."

Bill and Jimmy went over to the table where Jimmy's companion still sat. Bill nodded a greeting.

"What's your name, friend?" said the man at the table.

"Bill," said Bill, hoping that they would not ask him for more than that. He did not look either man in the face as he sat down.

"Bill?" said Jimmy. "How about that? This here's my brother. His name's Bill, too. Call him Billy. I'm Jimmy. Last name's Cook."

Bill looked up, astonished, but before he could say anything, Billy Cook was slapping him on the shoulder and talking.

"Well, Cherokee Bill, we're pleased to make your acquaintance. You done a good job on that fella."

Bill nodded, then said, "You Billy Cook, the . . . ?"

He stopped himself, embarrassed. He had started to ask, "Are you Billy Cook, the famous outlaw?" but realized in time that the question might not be appropriate. He was still new to this outlaw game and did not know all the rules. Jimmy came to the rescue.

"The notorious outlaw?" he said with a grin. "Yep. Damn right he is. *The* Billy Cook."

Bill reached his hand out toward Billy Cook.

"I'm right proud to meet you," he said. "Just call me— well, what you called me. I'm Cherokee Bill."

The Mexican Tattoo

It couldn't have been more than a couple of miles from the railroad tracks to his house, and he had never before thought it a long walk, but this particular December day it seemed the longest walk he had ever taken. The snow was only about four inches deep, but it was freezing his feet, even through the fancy cowboy boots he had purchased so recently along with his slick, black leather jacket. He had been proud of both purchases, but as he walked the long, cold two miles toward home, the boots looked like he had worn them for years, and the jacket wasn't in much better shape. It was cold, and he was tired. And what, he wondered, had it all been for? Slogging along in the snow, he thought back to the day he had left home and, with the last of his money, purchased a bus ticket. When the bus pulled out of the station at Okmulgee, he had sat there in his new boots and jacket and felt like he was riding out into a whole new world. A new life, it seemed, awaited him at the other end of the line. The other end was Odessa, Texas, where his older brother was a store manager for a small oil-field supply house, and he was certain that his brother could get him a job there.

He had to ask three different men in the streets in Odessa for directions to the supply house before he was able to find it, and when he did get to it, his brother wasn't there. He got directions to his brother's house from a man in the store and started walking again. When he reached the house, his sister-in-law answered the door. No, she said, he's not here, and she gave him another address and more directions. He walked again and finally found his brother in a small rented room—alone. It didn't take him long to realize that his unexpected presence was an embarrass-ment and an inconvenience, even an annoyance, to his brother, so he didn't bother to explain his reason for being there. He was just passing through, he said, on his way to El Paso. He would move right along. His brother saw through the ruse and gave him a five-dollar bill and a pocketful of five-cent cigars and wished him luck.

Back at the bus station, he purchased a penny postcard and wrote a short note to his mother.

"Dear Mama," it said, "I'm down here at Odessa visit-ing Jack and Lorraine. Don't worry. Everything's fine. Your son, Frank."

Frank had four dollars and ninety-nine cents, but he didn't know what he was going to do for more money or how long this would have to last him, so he waited until after dark, and then he climbed aboard a southbound freight train. (He had always wanted to hop a freight, any-way.) He managed to grab a few hours sleep, but he woke up before daylight and couldn't get back to sleep. He had crawled over the side of an empty coal car, and when the train had gotten well underway, he found that he was ex-tremely cold. He picked up his grip and climbed over the front wall of the car.

The car in front of him was a flat car. He walked its length unsteadily and made his way to the next one—a boxcar. Grabbing hold of the ladder that ran up to the top of the car, he swung himself around enough to look at the sides and see the doors. They seemed to be shut and locked. He decided to explore further, so he made his way up the ladder to the top of the boxcar. At first he stayed on his hands and knees, and he thought that perhaps he should make his way to the front of the car in that man-ner, but he had seen Bob Steele in too many western movies walk upright, even run, on the tops of boxcars, and he had to try. He stood up slowly. The wind was strong and cold. There was fine snow in the air, and the top of the boxcar was slick. He dropped back down to his hands and knees and crawled to the front, where he eased himself down onto the ladder at that end. With his grip held tightly in his left hand, he made a leap for the ladder on the next car. His foot landed on a rung of the ladder, but when his hand caught hold of the cold, slick steel, it slipped. He began falling backward between the two boxcars, but suddenly he was stopped with a jerk. He was hanging between the cars, his foot still on the rung of the ladder in front of him, and he felt himself being drawn upward and over the edge of the forward car by strong hands pulling at his leather jacket. When he felt himself secure on top of the car, his grip still in his hand, Frank looked up to see his rescuer. Sitting there beside him was a man, perhaps in his early thirties, not much larger than himself, but one of the hardest, toughest looking men he had ever seen.

"That was a close call you had there, boy," said the tough-looking character. "Why the hell didn't you drop that god-damn bag?"

"Hah, I don't know," said Frank. "I guess I just didn't want to lose it."

"It wouldn't have done you much good if you'd fallen under them damn wheels."

"No, I guess not."

Frank extended his right hand.

"I'm Frank Parris. I want to thank you for what you just did."

The man took Frank's hand and squeezed it until Frank thought the bones in his hand would break.

"Georgie Ballard," the man said. "Don't think nothing of it. I'm just glad I happened to be up here. Where was you headed, anyway?"

"I was in a coal car back there. It was cold as hell. I was looking for a warmer place out of this wind."

116

"Follow me," said Georgie, "but be careful, will you?"

"Yeah," said Frank. "For sure."

Frank followed Georgie to a boxcar, and they got inside and shut the door. Then Georgie built a small fire, and they hunkered over it.

"Where you going, kid?"

"El Paso."

"You got a job down there?"

"No."

"Relatives?"

"No."

"Well, me neither, and that's where I'm headed, too. These days, hell, you don't need no reason to go somewhere. Just going's reason enough, maybe, and besides, you never know what you might find someplace once you get there."

"I guess so," said Frank. "Do you mind if I ask you a question?"

"Shoot."

"How'd you get to be so damn strong?"

Georgie laughed.

"Just working, I guess. I been with the circus most of my life. Roustabout. Right now I'm with Ringling Brothers, except we went on strike up in New York. I figured, hell, if I was going to be sitting around out of work, I just as well be doing it down south where it ain't so damn cold. I wonder when I'll get that far south. It's sure cold enough here."

"Yeah."

"Where you from, kid?"

"My home's in Okmulgee, Oklahoma."

"Oka-whut?"

"Okmulgee," said Frank. "It's a Creek Indian name. Okmulgee was the capital city of the Creek Indian Nation up until about thirty years ago when they made Oklahoma a state and shut down our Indian governments."

"Okamawgee," said Georgie. "Okamawgee. Hmm. You an Indian, kid?"

"Well, I am part Indian," said Frank, "but it's Cherokee, not Creek."

"Hell. How about that? I ain't never knowed no Cherokee Indian from Okamawgee before. Say, if I was to stretch out here to grab me some shut-eye would I likely wake up with all my hair?"

"Oh, yeah. I don't scalp folks. Especially when they just saved my life. Besides, I'll most likely be asleep, too."

"Hey, kid, wake up. Come on."

Frank opened his eyes and wondered for a second where he was and who was shaking him and hollering at him. Then everything came back to him.

"What's wrong?" he asked, rubbing his eyes.

"This thing'll be pulling into El Paso pretty soon," said Georgie. "We don't want to be on it then. Them railroad bulls will be looking for travelers."

"What're we going to do?"

Georgie pulled the heavy door open and looked out.

"Jump," he said.

Before Frank had a chance to respond, Georgie flung himself out of the car. Frank jumped up and ran to the door. He leaned out and tried to see what had become of Georgie, but the track was curved, and wherever Georgie had landed, he was hidden by the angle of the cars. Frank tried to focus his eyes on a spot of ground to aim for, but it moved by him too quickly. He pitched out his grip, looked straight out, and jumped. When he hit, the ground seemed to race from under his feet, and he pitched forward and rolled over and over on the cold, hard ground. When he finally came to a stop, he looked up and tried again to focus his eyes on a spot—this time to stop his head from spinning. He found his grip, then started back along the tracks to look for Georgie.

They found a cheap room in El Paso, which Frank paid for, and just down the block they found a place where they could eat all the chili they could hold for ten cents. They

118

filled up on chili and went back to the room, where they discovered, to their discomfort, that they had no heat. There were two beds in the room, but to try to keep warm, Frank and Georgie slept together in the same one. They spent the next day walking the streets of El Paso rather aimlessly. They told each other they were looking for jobs, but there didn't seem to be any to be had, and to tell the truth, they didn't look very hard. They ate chili for all three of the day's meals, then they spent another night in the same bed together. In the morning, again, they went for a chili breakfast.

"You know, Frank," said Georgie, after he had eaten all the chili he could hold, "this ain't worth a shit."

"It's not exactly what I had in mind."

"You ever thought about joining the foreign legion?"

"What?"

"The foreign legion. You know, like Gary Cooper was in that there movie . . ."

"*Beau Geste.*"

"Yeah, whatever. You ever think about it?"

"No, I haven't, really. Why?"

"There's a French embassy down in Juarez, just across the border from here. They'll sign you up down there, and then they'll ship you off. What do you say? You with me?"

Frank thought for a moment. He looked at the chili left in his bowl.

"Yeah. Why not?" he said.

They crossed the border into Mexico that same morning but found the French embassy closed for the day.

"Well, since we're here, we might as well have some fun," said Georgie. "We can come back here and sign up first thing in the morning. Let's go have a drink."

Frank didn't drink, but he didn't want to tell Georgie.

"Okay," he said.

They soon found a place, and inside, Georgie ordered them each a beer. Frank paid for them and sipped at his, trying not to let his face show his distaste for it. Pretty soon Georgie got hold of a girl and slipped off to one side of the room. Frank managed to finish his beer, then he went outside and looked up and down the street. What to do while he waited? He noticed a tattoo parlor two doors down the street, so he went inside and had the man put one on his left arm. It was a kind of ribbon inside a wreath with "Mother" printed on it. He returned to the bar to look for Georgie.

Georgie was back and he had drunk a couple more beers in Frank's absence.

"Hey," said Frank, "let's go somewhere else."

They walked out into the street and began strolling along with no real destination in mind. A boy about ten years old ran up behind them. He tugged at Georgie's sleeve.

"Hey, mister, you want a shoe shine?"

"Naw."

"Come on, mister. You need a shine."

Georgie said, "Beat it, kid."

"It's only five cents. I give a good shine. Come on."

Georgie turned and smacked the kid across the face.

"I said beat it."

Suddenly everyone on the street seemed to turn to Frank and Georgie. Men who had been walking along in various directions, those who had been lounging against the sides of buildings, some who had been sitting on the sidewalks—they all seemed to turn at once. Some doors opened and more men came out of the doors.

"Chinga," someone shouted.

"Andale."

And one with some English said, "Get the goddamn gringos."

"Georgie?" said Frank.

"Let's get the hell out of here."

They ran down the street to the end of the block and turned the corner, the crowd right behind them. They darted across the street in the middle of the block and turned down an alley. The crowd was smaller, but still in pursuit. They ran a couple more blocks and turned another corner before finally eluding the angry mob.

"Come on," panted Georgie.

They ran another block and went around one more corner, then they walked an extra block for good measure.

"I got to take a piss," said Georgie.

"I'll wait here," said Frank, and he sat down on a bench there on the sidewalk. Georgie disappeared down an alley. On the other end of the bench from Frank was a man with a big belly, wearing a dirty, white suit and a broad-brimmed cowboy hat that was pulled down over his eyes. He appeared to be asleep. Frank tried not to look at him. *Hurry up, Georgie,* he thought.

"Hey, *gringo.* Where you get that jacket?"

"What?"

The man was not asleep.

"What did you say?" asked Frank.

The fat man turned to face Frank. He smiled.

"Where you get that jacket?" he said.

"It's my jacket," said Frank. "I bought it."

"That's a pretty expensive jacket. You sure you didn't steal that jacket?"

"I bought it."

"Well, you want to buy me a beer?"

"No, I don't believe so."

"You sure you don't want to buy me a beer?"

"I don't want to buy you anything." *Where is Georgie? Come on.*

Frank faced away from the fat man, hoping he would take the hint and leave him alone, but just then he heard the distinct sound of a double-action revolver being cocked. His head snapped back toward the fat man, who had scooted to the middle of the bench and was pointing a western-type revolver at Frank's head. It was cocked. Frank felt the sweat begin to pop out on his forehead, and he felt the sting of the new tattoo.

"You *real* sure you don't want to buy me a beer?"

Frank stared. He didn't know what to say. *Oh, Georgie.* Just then the fat man began to laugh. He lowered the revolver, and he laughed. He held his fat belly, and he laughed until he shook all over. Frank could feel the bench shaking from the fat man's laughter. Still laughing, the fat man pulled open his dirty white suit coat by one lapel to reveal a badge pinned just above the pocket of his grimy shirt. He was still laughing when Frank heard Georgie's voice behind him.

"What the hell's going on here?"

Frank jumped up.

"Let's go," he said, and he hurried away from the bench leaving Georgie to catch up with him and the fat man still laughing.

As Frank crunched through the Oklahoma snow in the field just a hundred yards or so from his house, he thought to himself how that had been the end of it. Of course, he had had to get back across the border, and he had ridden the rails back to Okmulgee from El Paso. He had even had one close scrape with the railroad bulls when they had stopped the train somewhere in Texas and searched it for travelers. Frank had ducked under a boxcar to hide from the bulls who were gathering up the travelers. He had been surprised to see that so many people had been in those boxcars. He heard one of the bulls say something about picking peas, and he saw them marching off at gunpoint all the travelers they had caught. The train had started to move again, and he had climbed back aboard. But none of that seemed important close to home. The whole adventure, or nightmare, had ended for Frank on that bench. Georgie had stayed. Perhaps he had gone back and joined the foreign legion. But Frank had gotten out. When he walked away from the bench and the laughter of the fat man, he had known that he was going to go home. He had started the walk then and there that he was finishing now in the Oklahoma snow.

Frank got to the back door before anyone at home was

awake. He slipped in quietly, made his way to his room, undressed, got into bed, and began drifting to sleep. Soon he became faintly aware of someone stirring in the house, then of his mother's presence in the room. However, he did not try to arouse himself, and she left again quietly. In the other room she met his father, and though she spoke in a low voice, Frank was awake enough to hear her say, "He's home, Ben."

Then her voice cracked just a bit as she finished.

"And he's got a tattoo."

Badger

Badger was many things. He was a full-blood Cherokee who could speak both Cherokee and English not excellently but well. He was a devout Baptist; however, he was a Cherokee Baptist, which is not to be confused with any other brand of Baptism on the face of the earth. He was an ardent fan of Cherokee gospel music and never missed an opportunity to attend a "singing." He was one of that fairly substantial number of Cherokees in eastern Oklahoma who, though they are not stomp dancers and often even consider the stomp ground to be the haunt of the devil, and though they are staunch Baptists, are still considered traditional, because they frequent Indian doctors and preserve many ancient Cherokee practices. But over and above all of these other things that Badger was, he was a policeman or, as he himself so lovingly expressed it, a "cop."

Out of uniform at a social event, Badger had once been introduced to some people, and those making the introductions had added the information that he was a policeman.

"Yeah," said Badger in his rough, low voice. "I'm the big pig. Oink. Oink."

The Cherokee country of eastern Oklahoma is infested with policemen. In any given city (small town, really) one is apt to run into representatives of the city police, the county sheriff's department, the Cherokee tribal police (officially named the Cherokee Nation Security Patrol), the Lake Area Security Patrol, the Oklahoma State Highway Patrol, the Oklahoma State Bureau of Investigation, and the Federal Bureau of Investigation. The latter two, of course, imagine themselves to be incognito, but more often than not, they are known and recognized by most people in town. The others are all uniformed. All are armed. Badger was a uniformed cop, a proud member of one of the previously mentioned agencies. The particular force, county, and city are irrelevant to his story.

Badger wore his uniform with great pride, and with even greater pride, if such is possible, he carried a huge .44 magnum revolver at his side. He had purchased the weapon with his own funds after finding the standard-issue side arm inadequate for, if not his needs, his ego. Badger's partner at the time he purchased the pistol, a young Creek Indian named Bowleg, was astonished.

"What do you need with a weapon like that?" he asked.

"We get some pretty tough characters around here," said Badger. "This'll stop them."

"Yeah, I guess," said Bowleg, shaking his head in disbelief.

Badger attributed Bowleg's incredulity to the fact that Bowleg was a rookie. Badger, a graduate of the American Indian Police Academy, fancied himself the only thoroughly trained police officer in the entire Cherokee Nation. He believed it was his duty to bring young fellows like Bowleg along. If they could tough it out and stick with him, he thought, one of these days they would be all right.

One night while making their rounds, Badger and Bowleg stopped by a local motel to check the lobby. There was a bar in the motel, and it was nearly closing time. A white woman in the lobby was staggering around and talking loudly. Badger walked menacingly toward her.

"Lady, I think you better go home," he said.

"Huh?" she said, turning her bleary eyes in his direction.

"I said you better get out of here if you don't want me to run you in. You're drunk."

"All right. All right," she said. "I'm going."

She made her way outside and to a parked car, but she soon returned to the lobby. She walked right past Badger and Bowleg and was moving toward a pay phone down the hallway. She stopped, looked at Badger, opened her purse and reached in with her right hand. Badger's right hand went for his magnum.

"What the hell are you doing?" said Bowleg.

"She's going for a gun," said Badger.

Just then the woman's hand came out of her purse holding a beer can.

"Well, she might have had a gun," said Badger.

For all this unintentionally comic posturing, Badger was not a man to mess with, even when he didn't have his magnum. On one occasion he and Bowleg had confronted a brawler who was even bigger and meaner looking than Badger. When the brawler challenged Badger's authority, Badger squared off and stared hard into the man's face.

"Ayuh jaduji," he said.

Then he swung his right fist into the man's forehead and sent him crashing to the floor unconscious. Later in the patrol car, Bowleg asked him, "What did you say to that guy?"

"Don't you understand Cherokee?" asked Badger.

"I'm Creek," said Bowleg.

"Oh, yeah. Well, I'll tell you an old Cherokee trick, boy. It don't matter how big or mean a man is. It'll work every time. You look right at a man and picture a rattlesnake right between his eyes. Really see it there. Then you tell him, 'Ayuh jaduji.' That is, you tell him, 'I'm your uncle.' Then you let him have it. One punch is all it takes."

"You're shitting me, man."

"You seen it, didn't you?"

One evening Badger called Bowleg at home and asked him to drive by his place out in the country and pick him up on the way in to work.

"My car's in the shop," Badger explained.

The next day Bowleg arrived at Badger's a little early, so Badger invited him in for a cup of coffee before they went to work. Sitting in the living room of Badger's "Indian house," in front of the wood stove on the concrete-slab floor, Bowleg sipped the strong, black coffee. It was full of coffee grounds, so Bowleg knew that it had been made in the Indian style, by dumping grounds into a pot of boiling water.

"What happened to your car?" he asked, trying to make conversation.

"I wrecked it last night," said Badger.

"Wrecked it?"

"Yeah."

"How'd it happen?"

"Well, really," said Badger, "it was early this morning on my way home from work. I went to make that turnoff to my road here from the highway, and that steering wheel just kept jerking back, like that, like someone was pulling on it, and I went down in the ditch. I was supposed to get killed."

"What? What do you mean?"

"Somebody's messing with me. I looked that car over and found the medicine. It was in a little sack tied onto the steering linkage."

"You mean someone's trying to kill you using medicine?"

"That's right."

"Who do you think it is?"

"I don't know. It could be anybody. But whoever it is, he's messing with the wrong man. I ain't putting up with it no more."

"You mean this has been going on for awhile?"

"Quite awhile. Old hoot owl hanging around my house. Things disappearing on me. Little things going wrong. This last is too much, though. I'm going to get him now."

"You been to a doctor?"

"Yeah. I got some stuff to protect me. You know, to protect my house. I guess it ain't strong enough, but the next will be."

They finished their coffee and went on to work. Badger said nothing else about his problem. When their shift ended, Bowleg offered Badger a ride home. Before they had arrived at Badger's cutoff, Badger asked Bowleg to take another road. Bowleg turned off, and the road soon dwindled to little more than a wide path winding through the woods. They rounded a corner and a small frame house appeared.

"Right here," said Badger.

There was an old man standing on the porch watching them pull into the yard. He was smiling.

"He's expecting me," said Badger. "Thanks for the ride. I'll find my way home."

It was two days before Bowleg stopped by Badger's house again on the way to work. They had had two days off and were going on the day shift, so it was early morning. As Bowleg pulled up in front of the house, Badger came hurrying out the front door.

"Come on," he said.

"Where?" asked Bowleg, as he shut off the ignition and opened the door to get out of the car.

"I think I took care of whoever was bothering me," said Badger. "Let's go take a look."

"Hold on a minute. What'd you do?"

Badger stopped and turned to face Bowleg.

"All right," he said. He pulled the .44 magnum out of his holster and flipped out the cylinder. He ejected an empty shell casing from the cylinder into his hand. He snapped the cylinder back into place and holstered the gun.

"See this?" he said.

"What'd you use that on?"

"You know that old hoot owl I told you about?"

"Yeah."

"Well, you know, you can't kill a *tsgili* with no ordinary bullet. You know what a *tsgili* is?"

"That ain't what we call them in Creek, but I know what it is."

"You know that old man over yonder where you took me the other day? He's a powerful Indian doctor. Well, I took him this here bullet to get it doctored, and when I got home, I put it in the cylinder so it would be the next round to come up for firing. Then I waited."

Bowleg listened intently, his eyes wide open, as Badger continued the story.

"Sure enough, that old hoot owl showed up again, but not until last night. The sun was already down when I heard him. I got my gun and come out here in front looking for him, but I guess he seen me. He took off and headed for the trees that way.

"Well, it was dark, and I lost sight of him, but you know, with these here doctored bullets, you don't even have to take aim. So I just pointed it off like this here and fired."

"And you want to go off down there and see if you hit anything?"

"That's the idea."

"Oh, hell, all right, but we ain't got all day, man."

They crossed a small field and went over a short hog-wire fence into the woods. Just across the fence the woods rose up the side of a steep, rocky hill. Badger went rapidly up the hill, and Bowleg followed, with a little trouble. *The old guy's in pretty good shape,* he thought. Badger disappeared over the top of the hill. Bowleg went faster, and when he reached the top of the hill, he almost ran into Badger's back. Badger had stopped. He was standing there, his hands on his hips, looking down. Bowleg stepped up to his side.

Lying there on the ground was the body of a little old woman, her face horribly contorted, as if in pain, and a great open wound in her chest. Bowleg gasped audibly at the unexpected sight. When he was finally able to tear his eyes away, he looked up at Badger, who was staring at the body and slowly and calmly shaking his head.

"It's my Aunt Ellie," he said.

"What?"

"I said that's my Aunt Ellie."

"You mean you killed your own aunt?"

Badger looked into Bowleg's eyes. His face had the expression of an exasperated parent who was tired of having to tell a child the same thing over and over again.

"I told you," he said, "nobody messes with me."

Calf Roper's House Guest

If anyone knew his real name to begin with, it was not long before they forgot it. He was known simply as "Weirdo" by one and all. The name had been given him by Calf Roper, who had decided on first glance that the alien from the North was just that—a weirdo. From then on Calf Roper never used the man's name. When the man was present, Calf Roper avoided calling him anything; when he was not present and Calf Roper needed to refer to him in conversation, he called him "Weirdo." Soon others picked up the practice, and except that they did not use it to Weirdo's face, "Weirdo" might as well have been "Weirdo's" real name.

Weirdo was a graduate student in economics at a northeastern university. He was supposedly engaged in research for his dissertation, the topic of which had something to do with the economic conditions of the Cherokee people in eastern Oklahoma. He had come to Tahlequah at the invitation of one of the tribal bureaucrats, a man named Cabbage, to conduct his research. Cabbage had a problem. He himself was out of touch with the people he considered "real Cherokees." In Cabbage's mind, to be a real Cherokee one not only had to speak only Cherokee but also had to be unemployed and live in dire poverty. He wanted Weirdo to experience living with real Cherokees while doing his research, so, naturally, he ruled out himself and his coworkers as hosts. But a happy coincidence came his way.

Calf Roper worked for the tribe, and he had a good job, but Calf Roper had just had it out with his wife. She was a white woman, and she stayed in the house and kept the car. Calf Roper continued to pay the rent and make the car payments. Calf Roper had a good job, but it was not so good that he could afford two fine homes and two good cars. He bought himself a used Pontiac station wagon for $400, and he rented a small house, which was not much better than a shack, in town. As soon as Cabbage saw the shack, he asked Calf Roper if he would mind putting up Weirdo during his visit. Not having met Weirdo yet, Calf Roper agreed. Then, when it was too late, he met and renamed Weirdo.

Weirdo was a white man. That much had been anticipated. But he was so very white. His tousled blond hair was so blond that it was almost white, and his pale blue eyes hadn't much more color than his hair. Weirdo was tall, and he was one of those tall people who seem to be always apologizing for his height by cultivating a peculiar stance that involves keeping the knees constantly bent, leaning slightly forward, and rounding the back and shoulders. Even for his height, Weirdo's feet were extraordinarily long. And to top it all off, his face showed a perpetual grin—not a smile, but a grin—as part of an expression that seemed calculated to openly announce eagerness and friendship to the world at large. In short, he was weird.

But Calf Roper had given his word, and Weirdo moved into the shack. He really wasn't much of a problem. No one would have been. Calf Roper did little in his shack besides sleep, and he did as little of that as he could get by with. He usually went directly from work to his favorite bar and stayed until closing time. In spite of his late hours, Calf Roper developed the habit of rising early so that he could escape the shack before Weirdo was up and about. So for a week or so, all Calf Roper saw of Weirdo were some unruly tufts of nearly white hair sticking out of the sleeping bag on the floor.

But one evening Calf Roper went by the shack to change his clothes before going to the bar, and Weirdo ambushed him.

"Do you mind if we talk?" he said.

Calf Roper felt sick.

"No, I don't mind," he said.

Calf Roper picked up his six-shooter from the wooden keg that served as his nightstand to make room for a six-pack. He put the beer on the keg and the gun on the floor. Then he stretched out on the canvas cot he used for a bed. Weirdo dragged up a folding chair and sat down. He seemed to poke his grinning face at Calf Roper.

"Do you want some tea?" he said. "I made some tea."

"Naw," said Calf Roper. "I'll just stick to this."

He popped the tab off the top of a beer can and took a long drink. He threw the tab on the floor.

"I hope you don't mind if I made some tea in your kitchen," Weirdo said.

Calf Roper said, "Hell, no, somebody ought to use the damn kitchen. Make yourself at home."

I wish he'd get the hell out of here, he thought.

"Hey, did you know about all that stuff growing out in your yard?" said Weirdo.

"What stuff?"

Weirdo jumped up and ran to the kitchen. He came back just as far as the doorway and held up in both his hands some sorry-looking, half-wilted pig weed.

"This marijuana," he said. "There's all kinds of it growing out there. It's just growing wild. Did you know it was out there?"

"Oh yeah," said Calf Roper.

"You don't mind if I use some?" said Weirdo.

"Help yourself."

"Wow. Thanks."

Calf Roper got up and walked to the kitchen door to peek inside the kitchen. There was pigweed hanging over the backs of the other three folding chairs. (Calf Roper had brought a card table and four folding chairs from his house.) There was pigweed laid out along the length of the counter. The doors to the wall cabinets were all standing open and draped in pigweed.

"Jesus Christ," he said as he walked back to his cot. "Is that what you wanted to talk about?"

Calf Roper stretched out again on the cot, and Weirdo resumed his seat and re-thrust his face at Calf Roper.

"No," he said. "I wondered if you would mind if I interviewed you as part of my research."

"What the hell," said Calf Roper. "Shoot."

"I was reading about the stomp dances."

Calf Roper thought, *What the hell has that got to do with economic conditions,* but he kept quiet.

"Do they still have them?"

"Sure. They still go on."

"Do you go?"

"No. I wasn't raised in a stomp-dance community. I'm an outsider at the stomp grounds."

"What would happen if an outsider went?"

"Nothing would happen. Nobody wouldn't beat you up or throw you out or anything. But they'd rather you didn't go. I won't even go. I'm Cherokee, and I won't go."

"Oh," said Weirdo, and for the first time since Calf Roper had met him, the grin left Weirdo's face for a few seconds.

"This marijuana will dry in a few days," he said, suddenly perking up again, "and we can smoke it."

Calf Roper said, "Yeah. I reckon."

He got up from his cot.

"Listen," he said, "I've got to go someplace. I'll see you later."

Really, Calf Roper had no place in particular to go. He just wanted out. He could bear no more of Weirdo. He left and went to a bar. He stayed out until the bars were closed and then headed back for the shack. About three miles out of town he had a flat tire on the Pontiac, but he didn't feel like stopping to change it, so he just kept driving. When he parked in the yard in front of the shack, he didn't even look at the tire. He went inside, stretched out on the cot, and went to sleep. The next morning he was up early as usual, but he didn't leave. He went outside to change the tire. Weirdo came out and found him there.

"Wow," he said. "What happened to that tire?"

"It lost its air," said Calf Roper.

"Yeah, but did you drive on it?"

The tire was an awful mess. It looked like a large, dirty shredded-wheat biscuit.

"Yeah."

"What's the matter? Don't you have a spare?"

Calf Roper let out an audible, exasperated sigh.

"I just didn't want to fuck with it at the time, that's all," he said.

"Wow," said Weirdo. "You're a real Indian. You just don't give a shit."

For the next several days Calf Roper again managed to avoid Weirdo. He did see him briefly one evening, smoking pigweed in his Dr. Grabo pipe with a strained and perplexed look on his face, but that was all. That was all until the morning of the final day. It was a Sunday morning, and Calf Roper had been out almost all night. He slept late. When he finally opened his eyes, he knew he had made a mistake, for there was Weirdo, his perpetual grin already set for the day.

"I got a tape I bet you'd be interested in hearing," he said.

Calf Roper muttered something inaudible as he pulled on his trousers. Weirdo raced into the kitchen where a small tape player lay on the card table. He punched a button, and Calf Roper heard the sounds of the stomp grounds.

"You hear that?" said Weirdo.

"I hear it."

"You know what it is, don't you?"

"Yeah, I know what it is. Where the hell did you get it?"

"I went to the stomp dance last night."

Calf Roper could scarcely believe what he was hearing. "You what?"

"I went to the stomp dance. And I danced, too."

Calf Roper put his face in his hands and closed his eyes. A grotesque vision of Weirdo appeared in his head, his long feet flapping around the fire, that sickening grin on his face. He imagined Weirdo offering everyone at the stomp ground pigweed. Just then the tape changed. There was talking.

"What's that?" said Calf Roper.

"Oh, I interviewed the people," said Weirdo.

"You mean you carried that damn tape recorder around out there and . . ."

Calf Roper was interrupted by the sound of a horn honking out in his yard. Weirdo ran for the front door.

"I've got to run," he said. "I'll see you later. I'm going to play stickball."

Calf Roper walked to the window and looked out. There was Cabbage in his car. Weirdo got in and they drove away.

"That stupid son of a bitch," said Calf Roper, and he kicked a beer can across the floor. Then he sat down and said quietly to himself, "I ought to kill the son of a bitch."

Calf Roper did not drink that day. He visited some friends briefly. He drove around. He was restless and irritable. He could not get Weirdo out of his mind. When evening finally came, Calf Roper did not go back to the shack. He was afraid he would see Weirdo, and he was afraid of what he might do when he did see him. So he went visiting and stayed so long with some friends that he was certain he had worn out his welcome. Finally it was late enough that Calf Roper figured Weirdo would be asleep, so he started for the shack, but on the way he had an idea. He stopped and picked up a six-pack.

When Calf Roper parked in his front yard he was sober

as a judge, but he pulled one can loose from the six-pack, popped the tab, and took a long drink. He let the beer run down his chin and onto his shirt front. He opened the glove compartment and removed his pistol, sticking it down in the waistband of his trousers. He opened the car door and then, open beer in one hand, six-pack dangling from his other hand, he got out and kicked the door shut. He drank some more beer, then staggered to the tiny porch on the front of the shack. Calf Roper stamped on the steps as noisily as he could, staggered back a few steps, and did it again. He fell heavily against the side of the house. Then he made a tremendous racket getting himself through the two ill-fitting doors. Weirdo was already in his sleeping bag. The lights were all out. Calf Roper belched loudly. He flipped on the light by the door. Then he went around the shack and flipped on every other light. He stomped and staggered everywhere he went, and he swilled the beer, and, now and then, he belched. He emptied the beer can in record time, threw it across the room and popped open another. He went into the kitchen, put a Waylon Jennings tape into the tape player and turned the volume up full blast. Finally, he went to his cot, banged his beer can down on the keg, pulled out his pistol, and sat down.

Calf Roper began to play with the gun. He cocked the hammer and then eased it down. He spun the cylinder. He twirled it around his trigger finger. And in between his antics, he gulped beer and belched. Out of the corner of his eye, Calf Roper saw some movement on the floor. Weirdo was easing himself down deeper into the sleeping bag. Soon not a single tuft of his hair was to be seen protruding from the bag. Calf Roper consumed the rest of the six-pack, then fell back on the cot into a deep sleep, ignoring the lights and the music. The gun was beside him on the cot.

When Calf Roper woke up the next morning, Weirdo and his sleeping bag were gone. There was a short, penciled note lying on the keg.

> Calf Roper,
> Thank you for all your help.
> The rest of my research has to be done
> in libraries, so I have to go.

The note was signed with a real name, but Calf Roper did not recognize it. He wadded the paper up, dropped it on the floor, and started to dress for work.

Calf Roper's Bandit Car

When Calf Roper and his white woman finally settled things between them and she left Oklahoma for good, Calf Roper moved out of the shack he had been living in and back into his house. But the house was empty, or nearly so. She had left him a couch and one chair in the living room, a chest of drawers in the bedroom, his books, his clothes, and a few old dishes. Calf Roper took the card table and four folding chairs he had used in the shack, his folding cot, and the portable cassette-tape player back to the house and bought a secondhand refrigerator. Then, from an ad he saw in *Penthouse* magazine, he ordered a king-sized air mattress to use for a bed, and that was it.

He was lying on the couch one evening listening to Willie Nelson sing "Whiskey River" on the tape player when the phone rang. Calf Roper picked it up.

"Yeah?" he said.

"What do you say, Osikid?"

Calf Roper recognized the voice and the mild Cherokee epithet.

"Cornbread," he said. "What's up?"

"You going to keep your house?"

"Yeah. I got no place else to go."

"How many bedrooms you got?"

"Three. All empty."

"You want a roommate? I'll pay half your rent."

"Sure," said Calf Roper. "Why not?"

Cornbread moved into the house and into the front bedroom right away. He brought a television set and a stereo with him, so Calf Roper figured he came out ahead on the deal. But Cornbread didn't pay half the rent. Cornbread was always working angles, and he usually came out on top.

"How's your Pontiac doing?" he asked Calf Roper one Sunday afternoon.

"It's okay."

"You want to trade cars with me?"

Calf Roper looked out the window at Cornbread's Maverick. It was a slick little car—dark blue with a white vinyl top. It had oversized tires to match its oversized engine. Calf Roper was thirty-five years old and had never owned a real hot rod.

"How do you want to trade?" he asked.

"Give me your Pontiac and six months' free rent and take over my payments."

"Deal," said Calf Roper.

Calf Roper enjoyed driving the Maverick. It had loud pipes and tremendous pickup. When Calf Roper stepped on the gas, he felt like he was going to wind up in the back seat. It was a real hot rod. He began calling it his "Bandit Car." He and Cornbread had gone three times (once sober) to see the movie *Smokey and the Bandit*. The Bandit Car fit right into Calf Roper's new image of himself. He had just recently been freed from a rather staid fourteen-year marriage, and he felt young and wild. He drove fast, drank hard, spent wildly, chased women (occasionally caught one), and carried a gun (sometimes two) wherever he went. Generally, he did whatever he felt like doing whenever he wanted to do it. Often he would arrive home late at night drunk and, if the Pontiac was there, announce his arrival to Cornbread by stepping out of the Bandit Car and firing three or four shots into the air. (Living out in the country allowed for a certain extra amount of abandon.) Soon Cornbread took up the same practice on nights when he arrived home later than Calf Roper.

One night Calf Roper was out especially late. He had been to a party in town and he was drunk. He did not realize how drunk he was until he found himself leaving the party and staggering to the Bandit Car, his head swimming. He fell into the driver's seat and searched for the keyhole. He rested his head for awhile on the steering wheel. Finally he started the car, roared backward out of the driveway, stomped on the brakes, then peeled out and headed for home. He knew he was drunk. He decided to take the back roads, which would keep him out of traffic and off the highway for all but the last few miles to his house. Calf Roper raced down the narrow, rocky, unpaved roads, over the hills and around the hairpin curves.

Just like the Bandit, he thought.

He also had the vague realization that if another car should suddenly appear coming from the other direction over one of the hills, he would probably be killed. The thought, however, failed to slow him down. He raced up a hill, and on the other side the Bandit Car left the road. Calf Roper felt a thrill as he flew through the air and then landed with a thud and kept racing. He rounded a curve, skidding and throwing dirt and rocks, and found himself on pavement. He began to open it up. Then he remembered that the pavement was a signal that the highway was just ahead. He remembered, but it was too late. As he took his foot off the gas, he saw the highway passing beneath him as he raced across it. He turned the wheel desperately to his left, managing to make the turn in time to race down the roadside ditch, just avoiding the fence beyond it. When he realized what he had done, he didn't bother with the brakes. He just drove the ditch a ways, then steered back up onto the highway, and continued on his way home. His heart was pounding from the excitement, and his head hurt from knocking the underside of the Bandit Car's roof several times when he had been bouncing through the ditch. Calf Roper drove home, parked, got out of the car, fired three shots into the air, and went inside and to bed.

The next morning, sober, he looked at his car. He could see no damage. The only visible evidence of his adventure was an abundance of long weeds hanging down from the front bumper and sticking out of the grill. The Bandit Car looked as if it had been grazing. But when Calf Roper got it out on the highway on his way to work, he discovered that the Bandit Car had developed a steady and rhythmic lurch to the right. Later investigation uncovered a broken shock and a bent frame. That had not happened to the Bandit Car in *Smokey and the Bandit* when it ran off the road.

About a week later Cornbread wrapped the Pontiac around a tree in Tahlequah as he was driving drunk late at night. His wallet with all his identification and a loaded .44 magnum pistol were in the glove compartment. An ice chest full of beer was on the seat beside him. Cornbread grabbed the ice chest and ran.

Calf Roper had his Maverick repaired and Cornbread bought a new car. Neither one did anything as dramatic as resolving to quit drinking, but their habits did change noticeably, and they did begin bringing their six-packs into the house unopened.

Bob Parris's Temper

"Grandma," said Calf Roper, "I found a newspaper story from the old Cherokee newspaper in Tahlequah. It was printed sometime in the 1890s. I don't remember exactly when, but it was about Bob Parris."

"About Bob Parris?" said Grandma. She spoke loudly and asked for almost everything to be repeated. She was ninety years old and her hearing had begun to decline, but overall she was remarkably healthy for her age.

"Yeah," said Calf Roper, "it was about Bob Parris, and . . ."

"Well, that was my daddy's name."

"Yeah, I know. That's why I noticed it, but I guess there were two or three Bob Parrises running around these parts at the same time, and they were all cousins or something."

"Oh, is that right?"

"Yeah, so I don't know if the Bob Parris in that story was your daddy or not, but it was about the right time, and it said that Bob Parris got into an argument over politics with a man named Bushyhead at a store over by the Arkansas line, and Bob Parris hit Bushyhead over the head with a log."

Grandma laughed.

"That was probably my daddy," she said. "He was always interested in politics. You know, he was real good friends with W. W. Hastings. That's who that Indian hospital in Tahlequah is named after—W. W. Hastings. Well, they was real good friends, him and my daddy. I saw an old woman I used to know when I was a little girl just a few weeks ago in a nursing home. Her mind is just about gone, and she didn't remember me too well at first, but after a while she did and she said, 'I remember you now. Your daddy was rich.' Well, my daddy was never rich, but I think that she had my daddy mixed up with W. W. Hastings, because they was such good friends. But he was always interested in politics, and I'll bet that was him in that story, because he had a real bad temper."

"Is that right?" said Calf Roper. He could sense a story coming from his grandma, and he wanted to encourage it.

"Oh, yes, he had a real bad temper. I remember one time when I was just a little girl—I don't know how old I was, but you know, he died when I was just ten years old. He was a real young man, just thirty-two years old and so handsome, but it had to be before I was ten years old, and it was when we still lived over close to Tahlequah, but I don't remember when we moved out to Lost City. I don't know just when it was, but I was just a little girl, and we had a big old hog out there. Anyway, I was outside of the house, and I don't know what got into that old hog, but he grabbed me with his mouth right around my leg, just right by my ankle, you know, and he dragged me underneath the house. You know there was space underneath the house. And he dragged me right under there.

"Oh, he was a big old thing, and I was just little, so before I knew what was happening, I was underneath the house, and that old hog had me by my leg."

"Grandma," said Calf Roper, "he might've ate you up, and then I wouldn't have no Grandma. Was he going to eat you up? What was he doing?"

"Oh, I don't know what was wrong with him. He never did anything like that before. I don't know why he did that, but anyway, I was just a hollering, and my daddy came out of the house and found me, and, you know, he just shot that old hog right then. He killed him."

144

Calf Roper waited for more, but no more came. Apparently, Gramdma was done with her story.

"Well, Grandma," he said, when he realized that she was done, "I believe I'd have done the same thing. That hog might've killed you."

"Oh, that old hog didn't know any better," said Grandma, "but Daddy just shot him dead. He had a real bad temper. That was probably him in that story you found."

Yes, thought Calf Roper to himself, *it probably was at that.*

His Grandma's Wedding

Calf Roper was looking at an old photograph of his grandparents. He was amazed at how young they both looked and at how beautiful his grandmother looked. The picture was printed on heavy paper. Its edges were a bit ragged and it was slightly yellowed with age. But Calf Roper thought it was a fine photograph. He looked at his grandfather's face and his clothing and tried to imagine him as a young Indian Territory dandy. He recalled the story his grandmother had told him about the time she had refused to go out with him while he was courting her, and how he would get drunk and ride his horse into town and shoot out all the streetlights. Calf Roper remembered her telling that story many times before his grandfather had died. She would tell the story on him and then laugh, and then Grandpa would say, "Now, Mama, you know that's not true." But Calf Roper knew that the story was true.

"Grandma," said Calf Roper, bringing his mind back to the present, "you sure are pretty in this picture."

"What picture are you looking at?" she asked.

She was sitting in the chair across the room from Calf Roper, so he got up to cross the room and show her the picture.

"Oh, that old picture," she said. "That was taken after we got married."

"Oh, really?"

"Yeah," said Grandma. "I was still mad at him, and

that's why I was looking like that."

Calf Roper looked at the picture again. She didn't look mad to him at all, just very formal, as folks in old photos always look—formal and beautiful and very young—but he didn't say anything about that. He thought for a few seconds.

"You just got married?" he said.

"Yes, and then we went over and had this picture made."

"Well, what were you mad about?"

"Oh, he just never did think about anybody except himself. He didn't worry about other people's feelings. I wasn't even planning on seeing him that day. The only reason I was dressed up was because I had a date with another boy that day to go to a dance, but before he came by to pick me up, your Grandpa came by the house. He just said, 'Let's go to town and get married.' I told him that I had another date, but he didn't even care about that. He didn't even care that he was making me stand that poor boy up, and that's why I was mad at him when that picture was made, and that's the reason I look that way in that picture."

Calf Roper was still puzzled.

"Grandma," he said, and his voice betrayed a slight exasperation, "how come you went and married him if you were mad at him like that? How come you went with him?"

"Well, if I hadn't," she said, "I knew that he'd a just gone on and got drunk and shot up the town again."

Old Joe

Old Joe was old. He had outlived two wives and now lived alone. He had children, but they were grown and had families and homes of their own. Sometimes they visited him on weekends or on holidays, but Old Joe lived alone. One of his sons, his youngest, had never married and did not have his own home, but he was seldom at Old Joe's house either. He was a hopeless drunk, and Old Joe never knew where that boy might be. Sometimes he would show up unexpectedly and ask for money, and if Old Joe had any, he would give it to the boy. Then the boy would leave immediately and spend the money in no time on a bottle of wine, and almost as quickly the wine bottle would be empty. Old Joe lived alone. He lived alone and took care of himself as best he could, for there was no one else to do it.

Old Joe's house was on top of a hill at the end of a windy dirt road a few miles off a two-lane highway and thirty miles or so from the nearest town. He had no car, and if he had, he would not have been able to drive it. Old Joe did not have a driver's license. He did not see very well either, nor could he read English very well. He could probably not have passed the test for a license. Even if he had the license and a car, he seldom had any money and would not have been able to keep gasoline in the tank. Old Joe usually stayed home. He stayed home alone.

To pass the time at home, Joe read to himself much of the time in his Cherokee-language New Testament. When the season was right, he walked in the woods near his house and gathered mushrooms or wild onions. He carried his water from a creek that ran nearby, and sometimes there was watercress to gather there. Once or twice a month, his married daughter would shop for him in town and bring the groceries out to his house and stock up his shelves for him, and she would sit and visit with him for a while on those occasions, but the visits were never long enough for Joe. The young ones were all so busy any more that it seemed to Joe they never had time to sit for long and visit. And when they did visit, their minds seemed to be someplace else. And they talked in English. Far better company was the deer that came out of the woods to visit with Joe when he sat in the chair out behind his house for hours, reading to himself.

But Old Joe did not feel sorry for himself. He had his routines and his pleasures. He took care of himself fairly well. Of course, he did not really wash his clothes as often as he would have liked and he didn't really keep his house as clean and neat as his wives had. There was little variety in his meals anymore, but they were well cooked, and he didn't really have much of an appetite anymore anyhow. Joe took care of himself fairly well, except in winter.

Winters in eastern Oklahoma can be very cold, with winds blowing and freezing temperatures turning cold rain to ice until the whole world seems to be covered with a gleaming layer of ice. Oklahoma winters are especially cold in one-room shacks that are fifty years old and huddled beneath the trees on the backroads of the Cherokee hill country. Joe's house had not a trace of paint left on it, if it had ever had any. Its siding boards were warped visibly and nails protruded from their ends. There were no screen doors or window screens. There was no insulation. Inside the house there was an ancient wood cookstove that provided all the heat Joe got in the winter.

Joe spent much of the winter in bed under raggedy-edged blankets.

One autumn afternoon as the air was just beginning to feel a little nippy, Joe was in his house boiling water in an iron pot on his cook stove, preparing to make some coffee. He took a handful of coffee from the can and dropped it into the boiling water. As he was waiting for the coffee, he heard a car coming up the road to his house.

"Now, I wonder who that could be this time of day," he said to himself as he walked toward the door.

His son who worked and his daughter who went to college would not be out on a weekday afternoon. No one would be driving the other boy around. Joe went to the door and opened it in time to see a fat white man puffing as he hauled himself out from behind the steering wheel of a long, fancy car. Joe didn't know one car from another, but he knew when one was fancy. The white man saw Joe standing in the doorway.

"'Siyo," he said. "Can you talk English?"

"I talk English," said Joe.

The white man came puffing toward Joe.

"Is this here your name and roll number?"

He held a paper out for Joe to look at it.

"Yes, that's me."

"Well, I work for the tribe, and we got a new program this year to help out our older Cherokee folks."

"You work for the tribe?"

"Yes," the white man said, grinning. "I'm a Cherokee."

"Oh," said Joe.

"Anyhow, we got this new program, and what we're going to do is we're going to buy brand new wood heating stoves for our older Cherokee folks who live on low incomes. We got all the information on you down at the tribal office and you qualify for this program, so I come out here today to find you so that I can let you know the boys will be out here to deliver a brand new stove for you."

150

"What do I have to pay?" asked Joe.

"You don't pay nothing. This stove is being bought for you by the tribe. It's one of the things your tribal government is doing for you. Now I've got the directions wrote down here, and I'll give these to the boys who deliver the stoves for us, and they'll bring your brand new stove on out here for you. Now what do you think about that?"

"Well," said Joe, tugging at the waistband of his khaki trousers, "I don't know. I guess it'll be all right."

As the white man who said he was Cherokee drove back down the hill, Joe drank his coffee.

"A brand new stove," he said to himself. "That tribe never done nothing for me before. Winter's coming on, though. A new stove would be good."

Six weeks later the boys came with the stove and Joe had forgotten all about it. He remembered, though, when they brought their paper to his door, checked his name, and said that they were there to deliver his stove. They were driving a big truck, and it took them some time to unload the big stove from the back of the truck. It was heavy. It was shiny. Joe watched as the two boys struggled to get the large stove into his small house. When they had finally placed it directly in the center of Joe's one room, they gave Joe some papers. The papers had pictures of the stove on them. Joe turned to put the pictures away, and when he turned back, the boys were gone. Joe didn't bother to hurry after them. They probably went back to their truck for the pipe and the tools they needed to install it, he thought. Then he heard the truck start, and he went to his door in time to see it drive off down the hill.

The boys never came back.

That winter, Joe kept a fire going in his old cook stove, and he spent most of the coldest days under raggedy blankets on his bed. And though it was a little taller than he would have liked, the heavy thing that the boys had unloaded on him was pushed over close to his bedside, and he had a place to set his coffee cup there beside the bed.

151

Wesley's Story

*Wesley Proctor was a storyteller in the great Cherokee tradition
of oral storytelling. More than once I heard him tell the following
tale to spellbound listeners. Wesley is no longer with us, and I
have retold this tale. Its form on paper is mine. The story, to me,
will always be Wesley's.*

Ira and Gary were walking along a dirt road. As they
walked, they talked. It was a dark night, and it was late,
but the two boys were in no hurry. They kicked at rocks as
they ambled along, and both of them were looking down
at their feet.

"You know," said Gary, "maybe we should listen more
to them old men."

"Maybe so," said Ira.

"I mean, I been told before not to go to the stomp ground
and especially not to get close to that fire when I been
drinking."

"Yeah," said Ira.

"I never thought nothing about it before, but, damn,
while ago, whenever we was going around that fire, it just
come right out and bit me. Damn."

"Yeah," said Ira, "we should listen more to them old
men."

"Yeah, I ain't never going back to no stomp dance, at
least, not if I been drinking, I ain't."

"Some of them old men are *tsgilis*."

"You don't want to mess with them," said Gary. "They can do things to you, and they can turn into owls or dogs or just about anything they want to."

"Yeah," said Ira. "I wish I could learn how to do that."

"Yeah?" said Gary. "Well, I don't know. I think it's scary. Well, I guess I'll be seeing you. I guess I better head on home."

They had reached the top of a hill where a large rock lay beside the dirt road. Gary's house was through the woods on the side of the road opposite the rock. There was a road that went to his house, but the path through the woods was a shortcut. Ira's house was on down the road a ways, so they parted company there at the top of the hill beside the large rock. Ira stood for a moment and watched Gary disappear into the woods. He was tired, but he wasn't in a hurry to get home. He started to sit down on the rock.

"Hey, watch out."

Ira screamed and jumped clear to the center of the road. He could feel his heart pounding in his chest. He turned around quickly and saw, sitting on the rock, with one leg crossed over the other, a little old man in khakis and a slouch hat, holding a walking stick.

"Oh," said Ira, "I didn't see you."

"Tsalagis hiwonisgi?" asked the old man.

Ira answered in Cherokee that, yes, he did speak Cherokee, and from there on the conversation continued in the Cherokee language.

"Did you mean what you said?" asked the old one.

"What?" asked Ira. "What did I say?"

"When you said you wanted to learn, did you mean that?"

Ira's heart pounded faster.

"You heard that?" he said.

"Did you mean it?"

Ira swallowed hard.

"Yes," he said. "I meant it."

The old man stood up.

"Meet me at this rock tomorrow night," he said, "at midnight."

Before Ira could answer, the old man was gone. Did he move quickly and quietly into the woods, or did he just disappear? Ira couldn't say for sure, but he went straight home and to sleep, and his dreams that night were strange.

The next day, all day long, Ira thought about the old man. He didn't know whether or not he should go to the rock at midnight. A part of him wanted the powers of a *tsgili*, but another part was afraid. There was even a third element that had become involved in the argument inside of Ira—something that probably resulted from his public-school education. He was not quite sure that he believed in the powers of a *tsgili*. Perhaps, as the schoolteachers said, it was all superstition after all. Ira was so troubled by his thoughts that he didn't eat all day. He had slept past lunchtime, and when supper was on the table, he told his mother that he wasn't hungry. Besides, she had fixed liver, and liver always made Ira queasy. Instead, he went out into the woods and sat down beside the stream and tossed pebbles into the water.

But when midnight came, he found himself standing in the road beside the rock.

"Nobody here," he said to himself. "I must be crazy."

Ira looked down the road to see if anybody was approaching. He looked in both directions. Then he went over to the rock, and, looking carefully at it first, sat down on it.

"'Siyo, I didn't think you'd come."

Ira jumped into the road. It was the old man's voice. He looked all around. He looked at the rock. There was no one to be seen.

"Where are you?" he said.

"Look up here," said the voice.

Ira looked up and spied there before him, on a branch above the rock, a large, old, long-eared owl.

"It's me," said the owl.

"Oh," said Ira, and part of him wanted to turn and run.

"Are you ready?"

Ira took a deep breath.

"Yes," he said.

"Then hop up here on this smaller branch just beneath me."

"I can't do that," said Ira.

"If you want to learn," said the owl, "don't talk back and don't ask questions. Don't speak unless you are spoken to. Just do everything I tell you to do. Now, hop up here."

Ira bent his knees slightly and his arms went back in preparation for a jump, but as they did, he felt a strange sensation and heard a fluttering sound, and he had wings that spread out wide as he felt himself rise lightly and gracefully to the small branch, which he then grasped with—his claws.

"I did it," he said.

He lifted one clawed foot to look at and almost lost his balance. He spread his wings. He turned his head around backward.

"I did it."

"Of course," said the old owl. "Now, listen. Do you see that lone tree out in the field ahead of us?"

Ira looked, and he could see over the patch of woods they were perched in and out into the field on the other side. He had never seen out into that field from the hill before, and he could see clearly even though it was dark night. It was wonderful.

"Yes," he said. "I see it."

"Watch me. After I fly to that tree and light in it, you fly after me and land on the branch just beneath me, just as we are here."

The old owl spread his wings and took off, and Ira watched him make a high climb followed by a beautiful, long glide to the lone tree in the field.

"I hope I can do this," he said.

He spead his wings and flapped them tentatively.

"Well, here goes."

He sprang from the branch and flapped furiously. He was off. He was soaring. He was overjoyed. He was actually flying. He went higher and higher. It was a wonderful feeling. When he thought he was about as high as the old owl had gone, he spread his wings and began the long glide to the tree. The sensation was magnificent. At the end of his long glide, he alit on a branch just beneath the old owl.

"*Osda*," said the old one, "now we'll go again. Look ahead of us. Do you see that tree there?"

Ira looked and farther across the field stood another lone tree.

"Yes," he said.

"Watch me. When I land, you take off. Land on the branch beneath me."

The old owl flew.

Ira watched him, anxiously awaiting his own turn to soar once again. When he saw the old owl land, he flew. The thrill was as great the second time as it had been the first. As before, he landed on a lower branch. The old owl was perched above him.

"Now," said the old one, "you see the hill ahead of us?"

"Yes."

"On the other side of that hill is another field. In that field is another tree standing alone. Beyond the tree is a house. When I vanish over the hill, you follow me. Land on the branch beneath me as before."

The old owl was off at once. As he dropped out of sight behind the hill, Ira began his third flight. His anticipation was intense. As he rose high into the sky, he saw the tree on the other side of the hill and the house beyond. He saw the old owl fly into the branches of the tree, and he began his dive. The leaves shook and rattled as Ira's claws grasped the branch just below where the old one waited in silence. The moon was high in the sky, and smoke from the house's chimney seemed to be rising to the face of the moon. The old owl pranced on his branch.

156

"Now," he said, "you wait for me here. Remember, you must do everything I say without question. Are you sure of yourself?"

"Yes," said Ira. "I'm sure."

Suddenly the old owl flew high into the sky. For an instant Ira could see his silhouette against the full moon. Then from where the old owl had been, a bright purple light flashed in the sky and streaked down straight into the chimney of the house below. Sparks flew out of the chimney, then settled. Again the smoke quietly ascended toward the heavens. The night was very still, and Ira felt a chill in the night air. He knew that someone in the house lay near death. He had heard that a *tsgili* lengthened his own life by stealing time—years, even hours, minutes, or only seconds—from people who were weakened by sickness or injuries. If the old one could steal even a few precious minutes from the dying one inside, his own life would last just that much longer.

"I wonder how long I will live now?" said Ira to himself.

Just then the purple flash shot straight up out of the chimney. It went high into the sky and seemed to explode in front of the moon, and out of the purple sparks that flew about the face of the moon, the old owl came flying back toward the tree in which Ira was waiting. As the old one returned to his perch, Ira saw that he clutched his branch with only one foot. In the other he was holding something. The old owl then reached forward and down with his head at the same time lifting his foot to meet his beak, and he ate of the thing he held. It was dripping blood. The old one held the bloody thing toward Ira, and Ira forgot that he was not supposed to speak until he had been spoken to.

"What is it?" he asked.

"It is life. It is liver. Take and eat."

Ira shuddered with revulsion, and then his weight bore down on the small branch that was supporting him and broke it with a loud crack. Ira dropped straight to the hard, cold ground and landed with a thud. As he sat up, he noticed his legs. He felt his arms. His feathers were gone. He was no longer an owl. He was once again—just Ira. He looked up into the tree, but his eyes could not focus very well in the darkness. He could not see the old owl.

Ira had no idea how far he had flown following the old owl that night, but it took him three days to find his way back home on foot.

The Endless Dark of the Night

They had just pulled out of their drive and onto the rocky dirt road that ran in front of their house, and Sky had only just straightened the wheels of the pickup when the headlights caught the small, red fox standing in the leaves beside the road. Actually the fox was mostly gray, but it was early March following a long hard winter in eastern Oklahoma, so the predominance of the winter coat made sense. The fox did not move. It stood there bathed in the pickup's lights, and it stared, it seemed to Sky, right at him.

"That was a fox," he said.

"A fox?" said Gay. "You sure?"

"It was a fox, all right. Just standing there looking."

Gay got real quiet. That worried Sky a little, because generally when she got quiet like that something was bothering her, and more often than not it would involve some belief from the old Cherokee ways—something, Sky thought, that she was afraid he would interpret as superstition. The silence didn't last long. It was broken by the kids.

"Did you say a fox?" said Chooj.

"That's what it was."

"Was it real big?" said Little Gay.

"No, foxes are little."

The conversation continued along those lines—kids' questions—and that was the end of it. But even while he was answering the questions, Sky was thinking about other things. He thought of his wife's silence. And he thought of how unusual it was anymore to see a fox in the hills of eastern Oklahoma. He also thought about what the Indian doctor had told Gay when she went to him because of the problems they were having with the kids. He had told her that somebody might be bothering them. He had said to watch out for any unusual sounds or smells or small, strange animals around the house. Sky tried to put the fox out of his mind, but he couldn't. The picture remained vivid.

It had happened on a Friday evening, and the next day Sky and Gay were surprised by a visit from their good friend, Deacon. They hadn't seen the Deacon for some time—in fact, he hadn't visited them since their move to the country. They were talking about life in the country—how good it was compared to life in town. Sky told Deacon about the time the little yoneg boy across the street from them had pushed Little Gay off her bicycle into a ditch and Gay had gone charging out into the middle of the street.

"You're nothing but white trash," she had shouted, shaking her finger in the little boy's face.

"I think the whole neighborhood could hear her," said Sky, "and there was nothing but white people all up and down the block. When she come back inside, I told her, 'we better move out of this neighborhood.'"

"Yeah," said Deacon, "it's a whole sight better to be living out like this here. Out with the deer and such."

"We've had deer right in our yard here. Walking right down the drive here. And just last night I seen a fox right out here on the road."

"A fox?"

"Yeah. Right down this road out here."

"Well," said Deacon, "you know what the old Indians say about that—whenever you see a fox?"

"What's that?"

"They say that whenever you see a fox that somebody's gonna die."

Tsgili, thought Sky, but out loud he only laughed.

"That's okay," he said, "as long as it's somebody on my list."

But the new information kept bothering him. Gay hadn't heard, so Sky didn't say anything to her about it.

It was three days later when he was driving to work that he saw the fox again. It was in the same spot by the side of the road, but it was lying in the dry leaves on its side. It was dead. He stopped the pickup and stared at it for a moment, then tried to shake it out of his mind and drove on to work. Three more mornings he looked at the dead fox there beside the road as he went to work, and still he said nothing. Friday night, right on time, Gay's ex-husband, the kids' daddy, came to pick them up for the week end. He was the one, Sky was certain, who was behind the *tsgili*. He wasn't the *tsgili*, but it was someone he was paying. That was certain. Ever since Sky and Gay had gotten together, they had both had the feeling that someone was working on them. They were also fairly certain who was paying for it and why and that whoever it was was working in the most sinister way of all Cherokee witchcraft— through the children.

Sky and Gay went to bed early Friday night and made love. Their lovemaking was always good, and they believed that it was a divine love—a preordained love. It was something powerful. It was strong medicine. It was sacred.

On Saturday they drove to the home of Gay's mother and spent the day there. It was late when they got home, so they slept late Sunday morning. Early Sunday afternoon, a nice, warm spring day, they were out behind the house. Gay was walking along beside the fence where it separated the backyard from the woods, and she spotted something. Sky was across the yard, by the back porch.

"Sky," Gay called. "Come here."

"Okay."

He stopped to light a cigarette, then walked toward her, but before he got halfway there, he saw that she was pointing to the ground by the back fence. He walked a few steps closer, then he saw it—a dead fox. It was smaller than the other one, and it seemed to Sky to have been dead a little longer. It was lying on its left side, exactly as the other one had been, and, like the other one, there was no blood—no indication of what might have killed it. It was strange. It was eerie. And it didn't seem to fit any known patterns.

If you see a tsgili, Sky recalled, in four to seven days, he'll die. The fox is dead. Right where I seen him. But I always thought that meant if you seen him in human form. Another thing. If a tsgili dies or gets killed while he's in some animal shape, he's supposed to turn back into a man after he's dead. And that down the road there's a dead fox. And then there's that second one. Sometimes they go in pairs. But still it don't all fit.

Sky had been so intent on the foxes that for awhile he had forgotten some other things that didn't fit. Like the time they had all been out walking—Sky, Gay, and the two kids. They had just gotten back into the drive and the kids had run ahead of them to the house. They had gone around the far side of the house in the yard.

"Mama."

"Sky. Come here. Look."

When Sky and Gay had arrived in the yard, there had been nothing there, but Chooj said, "It was a big owl."

"He was just sitting right there," said Little Gay, and she pointed to a spot in the middle of the yard.

"He just sat there looking at us."

That had all happened some weeks earlier.

Another thing had been the set of small animal tracks the kids had found in the fresh snow one morning that winter. They had come back into the house and told Sky. He had put a pistol in his belt and gone outside to investigate. He had followed the tracks from the small barn, which stood away from and facing the house, through the

162

yard and up to the front porch. From there they circled the house, going clockwise and coming right up to the house at each bedroom window. Sky hadn't been able to identify the small tracks.

And then there were the crows. On several different occasions, two very large crows had flown into the yard and made their loud *ga gas* as if they were taunting those in the house. Sky had gone outside with his rifle, but the crows always flew away before he got them. Sometimes they would come back, louder than before—purposeful, it seemed. And Sky was always suspicious of them when they came around.

What is that damn tsgili? Fox? Owl? Crow? Are there two of them? Are they dead? Or did they leave them foxes here to do something to us?

The next few nights Gay's sleep, as it often was, was troubled by bad dreams. Sky called the Deacon.

"Well," said the Deacon, "it sounds to me like someone's trying to do something to you, and he don't know too much about Indian ways. Or else maybe what you got's stronger than what he's got."

Sky felt a little reassured, but he still felt like he needed further explanations. He knew some Creeks at work, and since Cherokee and Creek ways are much the same, Sky told them the story of the foxes. The Creek woman looked serious for a few seconds after Sky stopped talking. Finally she spoke.

"You better go see someone," she said. "Within the month. Don't let it go by."

"I don't want to go to a Cherokee doctor," said Sky. "You never know who the other guy might be using."

"I know a couple of good ones," she said. "I can take you to one of them."

No more was said. No definite plans were made. But Sky stayed home from work the next day. The kids were at school, and Gay had taken the pickup to work, leaving Sky with the little Vega. And he heard the crows. Sky went outside with his grandfather's .22, but the crows flew away. Soon they returned to taunt him. Through his living room window he saw them in the field across the way. He went quietly out the back door and around the house, staying close to the house and hidden in the shadows of the trees. He saw one crow high in a tree top. It was a long shot, but Sky decided to take it. He put the rifle to his shoulder and sighted in on the crow, and he couldn't remember all the right Cherokee words, so he said them in English in a whisper.

> Instantly, the Red Selagwuchi
> strike you
> in the very center of your Soul.
> Instantly.
> Yu.

And as he pronounced the final syllable, he fired. The crow dropped. Sky thought that he had hit it, but then it began to fly. Perhaps he had wounded it slightly. Perhaps he had missed it completely, only frightening it away. *You can only kill a tsgili with a special, doctored bullet.* He kept watching, and a few minutes later he saw two large crows through the trees on the other side of the field—flying down close to the road just about where the fox's body lay.

He went back inside and got his .22 six-shooter. He put the belt over his head and his right arm through the belt so that the pistol hung to the left side of his chest, the butt toward his right. He lit a cigarette, put the pack and lighter in his shirt pocket, and took the rifle in his right hand. He went out again, this time through the front door, and he got into the Vega, started it, and drove up the road to the place where he thought the crows had been, but he saw nothing there—nothing except the fox. He backed down the road, stopped to pick up his mail, then backed down the drive, and parked in front of the barn. He opened the door but stayed inside and started reading his mail.

He had read all the way through the classified ads in the

newspaper when he heard the crows again. He put the paper aside and looked out across the field. There were two of them, and one was just settling down on a large rock at the base of a tree. Sky got out of the car and laid the rifle across its top. He took careful aim and repeated the ritual chant.

CRACK!

The crow jumped straight up and yelled.

AI!

It sounded almost human to Sky. It flew. His shot must have hit very close to it and stung it with dirt. Both crows were gone.

Sky went to the field to look for any evidence that he might have wounded the crow, but he couldn't find any. He sat down beneath a tree in the field to wait for them to come back.

"Come on, you damn *tsgili*," he said. "Come on."

He waited for an hour there in the field, but the crows did not come back. He did see them from time to time, but they circled far out around the field.

"Damn *tsgili*. Son of a bitches."

He gave up and went back into the house.

"Probably just some damn ordinary old crows, anyway," he said. "What's happening to me? I know there's someone messing around here, but I'm starting to see *tsgilis* everywhere. I can't let this happen to me. I need to go see a doctor."

When Gay and the kids got home, Sky didn't tell them about the crows, but he spent the evening in a deep sulk, and Gay wondered what was bothering him. That night, when he went to bed, Sky could hear, perhaps only in his imagination, he did not know, the faint *ga gas* of crows somewhere out in the endless dark of the night.